DAWN OF HAVOC

A Post Apocalyptic Survival Thriller

WORLD WITHOUT POWER

BOOK 7

RYAN CASEY

GET A POST APOCALYPTIC NOVEL FOR FREE

To instantly receive an exclusive post apocalyptic novel totally free, sign up for Ryan Casey's author newsletter at: ryancasey books.com/fanclub

CHAPTER ONE

"Are you ready?"

"Not really."

"Don't fuck with me. Yes or no. Are we doing this, or not?"

"If it were up to me, we'd—"

"Be sitting on our arses twiddling our thumbs. I know."

"I never said that."

"You didn't need to. I know you by now."

"You don't know a thing about me, Sam."

It was morning. The sun was low. An orange glow hovered over the industrial estate. Sam always liked these mornings, although they were supposed to be pretty foreboding, weren't they? What was the saying? Red sky at night, shepherd's delight, red sky in the morning, fisherman's warning?

The sky was red right now. And *really* fucking red for that matter.

It was a good job Sam didn't listen to any of that speculative, superstitious nonsense, wasn't it?

He'd been watching the industrial estate for hours now. No sign of movement. No sign of life. It felt like forever ago that he and

Seann decided to come back here to try and rescue Tara and to get their revenge on Kurt, too—even though it was only a matter of hours ago. He didn't want to waste any time at all. It was just... well. Running back into a heavily guarded warehouse where he'd previously been locked away and left for dead wasn't exactly an alluring thought—especially when he knew how lucky and fortunate he was to escape that place in the first place. Time was well and truly of the essence. But at the same time... they had to be careful.

But they were ready now. They were both armed. Found some old military rifles on the way down. Which was something of an ominous sign in itself. How often did you just run into rifles these days? Especially here in Britain? But hell, he wasn't in a position to overthink it right now. It was a lucky find. Not many bullets, but enough to award them *some* protection. A rifle *without* bullets was enough of a deterrent, for that matter. But who had dropped them? Someone from the warehouse? From the industrial estate? It felt the most likely option. But why?

But now they were here, now they were staring back at this hellhole they'd been unfortunate to call "home" up until very recently... it was safe to say the nerves were kicking in.

"If we get this wrong," Seann said.

"We won't get this wrong."

"But—"

"We've done enough talking," Sam said. "Enough speculating."

"It's good to be cautious."

"Not if it gets someone killed," Sam said.

Seann opened his mouth. He was well-built. Bearded. Longish dark hair, quite greasy. He had a bit of a mashed nose like it'd been broken quite a few times in his life. Looked like the sort of bloke who had been in quite a few scraps. Sam didn't know a whole lot about him, in all truth. They hadn't really spoken about personal shit. Every time Seann tried to, Sam kind of just shut off. He couldn't let his mind become clouded. He couldn't allow himself to become distracted from the task at hand. The sole task at hand.

Getting into the warehouse.

Rescuing Tara.

And fucking Kurt up.

He stood by the rear entrance to this warehouse that had looked ominously quiet since they got back here. There was movement around here initially. A few sounds, a few gunshots, a few cries. But for some reason, that seemed to have stopped. It seemed to have died down. Sam didn't know why. He didn't know what'd gone down here. Didn't really want to acknowledge the darkest possibility. He just had to hope it wasn't for any reason detrimental to him. And by detrimental to him, really he meant detrimental to Tara.

He stood there, by the metal door to the warehouse he'd been locked up in. He listened. Listened for footsteps. Listened for voices. But he couldn't hear a thing. Which just creeped him out even more.

The smell... it was bad even from out here. That distinctive smell. Shit. Meat. Rot. All the worst smells, combined into one awful cocktail. A smell that would never leave him. A smell he'd never be able to run and hide from. A smell that would always bring back the traumatic memories of being locked up in here. Always.

But he had to look past that right now. He had to look past the smell, and he had to look past the awful taste in his mouth.

He had to find Tara.

He clutched his rifle. Stared at Seann, who held on to his.

"Ready?" Seann asked.

Sam took a deep breath. Nodded. "Ready."

And then he booted the door open and stepped inside.

The dark, dingy corridors of this industrial estate warehouse were just as Sam remembered. The grey walls. The broken old light bulbs dangling from above. And that smell he'd mentioned, even worse now he was inside.

Only something *was* different.

The bodies.

Not the dead bodies that these cannibalistic fuckers used to hang up as meat. It wouldn't be a surprise to see those anymore, as depressing a fact as that was. But there were other dead bodies. People slumped against the walls. Blood smeared across those cracked walls. Bulletholes. And bulletholes Sam was pretty sure weren't here when he was walking away from this place.

"What the fuck?" Seann said.

Sam held his rifle and kept walking. He saw these bodies against the wall. All of them slumped down there, arms twisted, legs contorted. The bulk of them lying face flat in a puddle of their own blood. Like they'd been trying desperately to get somewhere. Or to get *away* from something.

"Shit," Seann said, his voice echoing. "These—these are Kurt's people."

And Sam noticed that, too. Some of them, anyway. They weren't just the escapees. Some of them... they were Kurt's people. What the fuck had happened here?

But at the same time, he couldn't allow himself to speculate. He couldn't let himself get carried away. He needed to keep going. He needed to find Tara.

"When—when did this happen?" Seann asked.

Sam didn't respond. He focused on the door ahead. The door to the main warehouse area. But as he walked down there, he couldn't shake the feeling that he would find something he really didn't want to find.

"Shouldn't we check..." Seann started as he opened one of the side doors. "Fuck," he said.

Sam turned around. A ghastly smell filled his nostrils. The sound of flies buzzing, ringing in his ears. It didn't take him long to see why. The meat hooks. Greyish meat hanging down from those hooks. Looked like some of the meat had gone off. Smelled like it, too.

He saw that meat in there, and he knew what it was. Human meat. Flesh. These people. These poor fucking people. He just hoped and prayed the same fate hadn't befallen Tara. But the signs weren't looking good right now.

"Come on," Sam said, turning around, heading further towards that main door, into the belly of the beast.

Seann followed closely. The pair of them walked up to that door. Stopped right in front of it. That tension that followed them outside joining them here, too. Because everything was so quiet. Everything was so silent. So ominous. So... dead.

"You sure you want to—"

"I'm sure," Sam said.

Seann opened his mouth. Went to say something. Then just nodded. "Whatever we find," he said. "Let's just be careful. Okay?"

Sam turned around to the door. Took a deep breath. Held his rifle tight.

And then he opened the door to the main warehouse.

It was just as he remembered when Kurt walked him in here that day to psychologically punish him by making him speak with Tara. Only, again, there was a big difference.

"Fuck," Seann said, covering his mouth and heaving.

Fuck indeed.

Because in this room, in this warehouse, everyone was dead.

Kurt's people. The people who had been tied up as prisoners. Everyone.

Bullet holes in their heads, piercing through their bodies.

Lying flat on the floor.

He listened to Seann vomiting as he walked around the room. As he looked at the bodies. As he looked at the faces of each and every one of them. People who had been captured. And people who had *done* the capturing. Each and every one of them, just making sure. Just seeing for himself, for definite. Because whatever had happened here... it'd happened here recently. Very recently indeed.

And whatever happened here... he needed to know Tara hadn't been caught up in it. Even though it depressed him to admit that seemed like the likeliest option right now.

"Sam," Seann said between bouts of vomiting.

But Sam wasn't giving up.

He walked around the warehouse. He looked at every single one of them. Holding his rifle. Tension gripping his stomach.

"Sam, it's—it's too late," Seann said.

"It's not too late."

He kept on walking until he'd fully circled the perimeter. And then he walked around it again, looking at everyone even more closely.

He walked until he finished searching again, when he stopped in front of Seann. Vomit trickling down his face.

And then he swallowed a lump in his throat.

"She's gone," Sam said. "Kurt's gone. They're... Wherever they are, they aren't here. They're... they've already left this place. They've gone."

CHAPTER TWO

"I don't know, Sam."

"What don't you know?"

"I just... I just think you're getting carried away."

"Carried away?"

"Just because you've seen movement over here doesn't necessarily mean it's—"

"I know what it does and doesn't mean. I'm not thick, okay?"

"I didn't mean—"

"Let's just have a look," Sam said. "And if you don't want to join me, then that's up to you."

Seann shook his head. Sighed. "You say that like I have a choice."

Sam looked over towards the petrol station across the road. The weather was shit. It was late summer. Felt like autumn was creeping up a little early. Pissing it down. Grey skies. Lots of flooding in the streets. Reminded him of the beginning of this entire shitshow. Fuck, it seemed like an eternity ago. A whole other lifetime. It felt like so much had happened since then. Like so much had changed since then. Hell, he figured it had.

The petrol station looked like any other: abandoned and

falling to pieces. Same went for the rest of the street. It was ghostlike. So quiet. So silent. Not even any birdsong here, as if they knew there wasn't much in the way of food for them anymore—the seagulls, anyway. He could see the cars lining the streets. Could see the moss growing over them. He could see the smashed windows of the terraced houses and the graffiti smeared across the walls. The street lamps that had fallen down. The adverts for movies on the sides of double-decker buses. It was like standing in a history museum, in the middle of an exhibition, and looking back at the world as it used to be, as everything manmade rusted and withered away, and nature tightened her grip again.

Which was a shitter. Weeds everywhere. Sam was always getting tangled up in them and making a dick of himself.

But irritating weeds aside, in a way, it was kind of beautiful, too. Seeing the insects buzzing around, and the bright green grass growing through the cracks in the concrete. Seeing the bees flying from flower to flower. You could just about hear them if you really listened, a background hum of nature replacing the crackle of electricity of old. And it was peaceful. It brought a sense of ease. A reminder of a summer's day in the countryside, away from the smell of petrol and the sound of busyness and just *one* with everything. Like a Buddhist pizza.

Sam found himself losing himself in those sounds. He felt the cool breeze against his skin and smelled the petrichor in the air—the smell of the earth after rainfall on a warm day or after a storm. And he felt even more relaxed for a moment. Even more at peace.

And then he turned his attention back to the petrol station.

He'd seen someone. Movement. Looked like a woman, walking in through the smashed front windows of this place and disappearing into the darkness. And even though he knew the chances of it being *her* were slim... as long as she was out there, he couldn't give up. He couldn't discount anything. He couldn't just accept Tara was gone completely.

He hadn't found her in the warehouse that day a month ago.

And sometimes, he wondered whether Seann wished they had. Because that unknowing. That uncertainty about what'd happened to her and where she'd gone. As long as there was that uncertainty, Sam couldn't let go. And sometimes, that took its toll.

He walked across the petrol station foyer. Past the cars that were parked up here. The bulk of the petrol had been drained from the pumps, but there were still a couple of hoses dangling from these cars. Journeys in the storm that had begun, but journeys that were never concluded. You never got desensitised to that. You never got over the sheer horror and panic people must've felt when they realised that not only was the flooding horrendous, but the power was gone, too. That moment when life's stabilisers tumbled away, and you realised you were well and truly on your own. It was scary enough for Sam, and he knew his stuff about survival and EMPs and shit like that. So God only knows what it must've been like for an average family.

"Just keep your guard up," Seann said. "We don't want a repeat of what happened in Taviton."

"Taviton was well out of our control."

"No," Seann said. "We sneaked into a building where you thought you'd seen movement and almost got our arses killed by raiders."

"You're being dramatic."

"Dramatic? Try telling that to my almost-killed-arse."

Sam shook his head. Looked at the smashed glass, at that window into the darkness. He didn't want to overthink things too much. He didn't want to entertain the possibility that it might not be Tara. That he might never find Tara again. That he might never get the revenge on Kurt he craved. Because that possibility was painful.

And there was the small matter of Rebecca and Leonard out there, too. And Harvey. His dear fucking dog. Wherever they were, he hoped they were okay. He hoped Claude was okay and

Marky was okay. He hoped they'd found the safety and the shelter they needed.

But they were strong. He had faith in them. Safety in numbers.

Tara, on the other hand... he was worried about.

Very fucking worried.

He took a deep breath, and he knew there was no time to waste. And that there was no point in standing around.

And then he climbed in through the smashed glass and into the darkness.

The petrol station was in a bad way. The shelves that used to house all sorts of snacks had collapsed onto the floor. There was a horrid smell in the air like rotten eggs. Something on the wall too, which looked like smeared shit.

And then there was the sound.

The noise, right at the back of the petrol station. Right behind the counter.

Movement.

Sam swallowed a lump in his throat. He stepped closer to that movement, rifle in hand. He pictured Tara curled up there. He pictured helping her to her feet and telling her everything was going to be okay. It seemed far-fetched. It seemed unrealistic. But it was a possibility he had to hope for. That he had to cling on to.

He stepped around the counter and pointed his rifle at the movement when he saw her sitting right there.

She was small. Thin. Barely anything to her. Chunks of her dark hair were missing. Her face was covered in nasty, angry sores. Her teeth were all chipped and yellow.

And she was injecting something into her forearm with a dirty needle.

She looked up at Sam. Looked up at him with distant eyes. Greasy hair clinging to her face.

"Go away," she said. "Leave... leave me. Leave me."

And as Sam stood there, realising this woman wasn't Tara or

anyone he knew at all, just a poor junkie somehow still holding on, he wanted to help her. Because it just felt... unfair. It felt like she could be doing so much better than she was, even in a world that had gone to hell. He felt like he was abandoning her, leaving her behind.

"Go!" she shouted. "Go!"

He stood there. Rifle in hand.

Then he swallowed a lump in his throat and took a deep breath.

He turned around and walked out of the petrol station, away from that poor woman.

There was nothing he could do for her.

This was life and death in the apocalypse now.

CHAPTER THREE

Sam walked down the empty road and never for a moment stopped searching for Tara.

It was afternoon. The sun was beaming down from above, real bright. It felt warm. The rain had stopped by now, at least. That was something. There was still a little water on the road, though. His feet felt damp. His boots must've split. You don't notice this shit in the middle of summer when you're not getting all that wet. Hell, it was easy enough to find another pair. There were plenty of old shops around. Failing that, there were plenty of abandoned houses around.

Damn, if he was really desperate, he could take a pair of shoes off a dead body. There were plenty of *those* around, too.

It was late summer. An autumn chill was in the air. Felt like it was on the horizon and getting closer. He'd been travelling with Seann for the best part of a month now. They hadn't run into any major trouble together. The occasional looter and drunk. Some nasty group holed up in a shopping centre who were really pretty damned trigger-happy. But really, nothing out of the ordinary. *Everyone* was kind of trigger-happy these days. That was pretty understandable, really. Living in a world like this didn't make for the most trusting environment.

All around, the familiar sights of degradation and decay. Although Sam noticed things turning a little. Nature taking over even more. Weeds growing over the abandoned cars. Moss creeping up the buildings lining the streets. Humanity might've made its mark on the planet over so many damned years, but it wasn't taking nature long to take back control. Made you realise just how futile it all was when it all came down to it.

He listened to his and Seann's footsteps against the cracked, crumbling concrete. He was always listening. Any sound, anything out of the ordinary, and it could be someone dangerous. It could be someone who posed a threat. Or more important than that... it could be Tara.

He thought about Tara, and he felt guilty. Not just for what happened to her: ending up trapped with Kurt while everyone else got out of that godforsaken hellhole. But also because it reminded him of the other people he cared about out there, too. Leonard. Rebecca. Harvey, his loyal pup. And then Marky and Claude, too. Here he was, travelling with this man he barely even knew even after all this time together. And he still hadn't found any trace of any of them.

And even if he did, he knew he couldn't give up until he found her.

Until he found Tara.

He wouldn't rest until then.

"Used to be a nice town, this. Back in the day."

Sam heard Seann speak, and instinctively, he rolled his eyes. Didn't say anything back to him. Not a word. He never was one for small talk. And besides. Any moment chatting to this bloke could distract him from the task at hand.

But Seann didn't seem to get the message from Sam's silence. "I visited here once. When I was younger. The castle's a really nice place. Some nice cafes. Decent bars, too. Although I always was more of an introvert."

"Is there a point to your rambling?"

"'Rambling'?" Seann said. "Wow. You really know how to make friends, don't you?"

"Do I look like I'm here to make friends?"

"No. That's exactly the point I'm making."

Sam sighed. He didn't see much point in arguing. If Seann wanted to witter on, he could witter the fuck on to his heart's content. He didn't like him. Found him annoying. Appreciated he'd risked everything to help him rescue Tara, sure. But that was a month ago. If Sam knew a month ago just how fucking annoying this guy would turn out, he wouldn't have even entertained his offer.

"How far do we take this?"

Sam stopped. Sighed. "How far do we take what?"

"This... this road."

Sam shrugged. "As long as it goes on. I thought you were the expert about this place, anyway?"

"Not this *literal* road."

"Oh. I mean, you said 'road'. So don't blame me for getting that wrong."

"I mean... I mean this journey, Sam. This... this search. How long do we keep on going when... when the end result is always the same?"

Sam tasted bitterness in his mouth. So that's what this bastard was suggesting? Abandoning the search? "We keep on going until we find her."

"But what if we—"

"If you want to give up the search, you can," Sam said. "I appreciate your help. Really, I do. But there's always an out for you. I've always been clear about that."

Seann sighed. "Don't be like that."

"Then don't make shitty suggestions."

"I just... We've heard all sorts of whispers. Communities. Maybe—maybe we'll find her in one of those communities. And if we don't—"

"You want to find a community so you can convince me to stay there. So we can get there, and you can be all like, 'oh well, we might as well stay here.' *Not* because you think we might find Tara there."

Seann shook his head. "Sam, don't—"

"You've... you've got a choice. Keep walking. Keep searching. Or go your own way. But I know what I have to do."

Sam started walking again. He felt pretty pissed. He hoped he'd said enough to shut Seann up. But shutting Seann up was no easy feat, so he didn't have his expectations too high.

"There's other people out there," Seann said. "People who as far as we're aware, are alive. People who care about you. People you... people you walked away from. And people I'm pretty sure would love to see you again."

Sam stopped. He looked back. Narrowed his eyes. "Walked away from them?"

Seann lowered his head. "I probably worded that—"

"If you're talking about Rebecca, then don't you dare say another fucking word."

"But it's true, isn't it? You walked away from them for Tara. And I don't blame you. I would've done the same. But—"

"One more word from you, and I'll put you in a fucking hole in the ground. Understand?"

"Tara's gone, Sam—"

"Not *another* word. Do you understand?"

Seann stood there. He looked like, rare as it was, that he was legitimately out of words. He nodded. Lowered his head again. "I'm just worried in trying to find a trace of her that you're going to lose yourself."

"You let me worry about me."

Sam turned around. He walked away. He didn't know if Seann was still following. Truth be told, he didn't really care.

But as he walked, tears stinging his eyes, he couldn't escape those words Seann said to him.

I'm just worried in trying to find her that you're going to lose yourself.

But also something else he'd said.

People who care about you. People you... people you walked away from. And people I'm pretty sure would love to see you again.

He thought about Rebecca. He thought about Leonard. And he thought about Harvey, Marky, and Claude.

And wherever the fuck they were, he hoped to God they were okay...

CHAPTER FOUR

Rebecca wasn't sure how long she'd been walking, but she was beginning to lose all hope.

It was late afternoon. It'd just poured down earlier, and she was completely drenched. But the sun was out again, which helped. The weather was all over the place lately. And it made her anxious. At one point, it felt like summer might last forever. But a lot had happened since Keswick. A lot had changed. And that realisation that sooner than anyone expected, winter would be upon them all... yeah, that was a terrifying fucking thought.

She saw the trees all around her. Saw Harvey walking along up ahead. He seemed a bit sheepish. He had been this last month since finding Leonard again. Leonard said Murph died and that Harvey was missing him. Rebecca hoped that was the case, and he wasn't just ill. She wasn't sure this group could take any more loss. It'd had to deal with enough loss already.

She listened to the wind blowing against the trees. She could hear birds singing overhead. That was always a good sign. It meant there was no one close. Or was that a bad thing? In some ways, Rebecca wanted to avoid any other survivors. The run-in with Kurt and his cannibals and the hellish days she'd spent trapped there... fuck, that was enough to prompt a lifetime of trust issues. And she knew there were plenty more people like him out there. Plenty more groups like his.

But then she knew not everyone was a psycho. There were good people out there. There *had* to be good people out there. Because this wasn't some sort of overblown TV drama. Not everyone was rotten. There was goodness out there. She'd seen it. Lately, she'd just been... unlucky.

But it felt like that goodness was growing fewer and further between.

She felt a little tightness around her right hand, looked down, and saw Leonard by her side. Sometimes, just seeing her son right beside her, it made her wonder if she was dreaming. If she was still trapped in Kurt's warehouse, and she was picturing a perfect life. Imagining her greatest dream. Because she'd lost Leonard. She'd lost him months ago when Southfield fell. And now... now, he was here. Now, she was reunited with him again.

She looked down at him. Saw the way his head was slumped. Saw how exhausted and frail he looked. But also how he always lifted his head up, no matter what. He didn't mope. He didn't let the horrible circumstances they were in get to him.

He was such a strong kid.

A true survivor.

And just knowing how hardened he was... it made her feel guilty. Because she wanted her boy to be having fun. She wanted her boy to be enjoying his life. She didn't want him being forced to live a life of worry. A life of panic. A life of dread.

But he was here. And she was holding his hand. And that was more than most parents or children could say. It was a cruel world. She was so lucky she still had him.

She glanced past him for a second, over at Claude and Marky. Claude wasn't much of a talker. He was stoic. An emotional rock. Which was exactly what was needed right now. 'Cause, tough as she was, she got emotional sometimes. Not that she was remotely weak. She was sure Claude had his moments, too. He was just better at masking them than she was, sometimes.

Marky... Marky was quiet. He always had this wide-eyed stare to him. Of course he was quiet. He'd been through hell. He'd lost his mum, then his dad. He'd settled into a new home, which fell apart. He'd been kidnapped. He'd watched his sister die. And then he'd been kept prisoner in that awful place for God knows how long. Those were trauma wounds that just didn't heal, no matter how hard you tried. Especially since Tara was the woman who'd taken him under her wing and treated him like she would her own—and now she was gone, too.

But as much as he was suffering too... he was here. They were all here. And they were all close. And that had to be appreciated. It might not feel like much. But it was everything. Absolutely everything.

Only...

She looked over her shoulder. Back into the woods. She thought about Sam. And then about Seann, who went with him. She thought about Tara. She wondered where they all were. She wondered if Sam had got what he wanted. Whether he'd saved Tara. Whether he'd got the revenge he wanted over Kurt. She hoped so.

And as she walked, she wondered another thing, too. Something that made her knot up inside.

She wondered if she'd ever see Sam again.

She took a deep breath. Swallowed a lump in her throat. It hurt. Of course, it hurt. But they'd done their best. They'd done their very best. And that was what counted more than anything. In the end, that was all anyone ever really had. Right?

She turned around, and she kept walking, kept wondering where they were going to go next, where they were going to end up. Keswick? No. Keswick wasn't safe anymore. Keswick had fallen long ago. There was nothing left for them back there. She and Claude might've forged a bond there—a bond that she felt equally guilty and also happy about. But that place was gone. It was dead. It was a memory in a sea of so many memories.

She walked further when she saw something painted on a tree up ahead.

Three initials.

NRS.

And then an arrow, pointing ahead.

And a note underneath.

Safe haven.

"What do you think?" Claude asked.

Rebecca looked at those initials. And at that arrow. She didn't know what it meant or where it led. But she knew one thing. They needed something right now. They just needed something.

She took another deep breath, tensed her fists, and then she nodded.

"We have to try," she said.

Claude nodded back at her. "Yeah," he said. "We do."

She looked down at Leonard. Squeezed his hand. He squeezed it back.

And then she turned ahead again.

"Come on," she said. "Let's... let's see what we can find."

And then, together with her family, she walked.

Rebecca was so grateful to be reunited with her son and for these people she was with—and this dog she was with.

But she could never stop looking over her shoulder and thinking about Sam, Tara, and Seann, and praying that one day, they would walk through those trees and back into her life, all over again...

CHAPTER FIVE

Sam sat in the darkness of the abandoned house and knew he should probably get some sleep. But sleep just didn't come easy these days. Not one bit.

It was late. Middle of the night. It was still outside. The wind and rain had stopped. All Sam could hear was the silence. Which was ideal, really. He preferred the silence. It meant he could hear someone approaching from miles away. It meant that if anyone was out there, he'd hear them, and he'd know exactly who they were before *they* knew about him.

And it meant that if Tara passed by here, if Kurt passed by here... he'd hear them.

He had to believe that.

Even if it felt like believing a fairytale at this stage.

He looked around this dark, dusty lounge. There was an old TV set in the corner. One of the old CRT types. It looked ancient. Honestly, Sam would be surprised if it'd still worked even before the blackout. The carpet in here was all red and green patterned, trodden down after years of usage. The sofas were all sunk in the middle. There was an oxygen tank beside one of the chairs and a mask lying limply on the floor beside it. Stacks of

Daily Mail newspapers towering up on the side table, the cross-words completed in every one of them.

He pictured the people who must've lived here. He always pictured the lives of people. It was an automatic thing he did in this world. A way of staying in touch with the tragedy of what'd happened. Of never losing sight of your own humanity. And in this place? In this place, he pictured an old couple. He pictured them sitting inside most of the day, except when they had to leave to collect their pension. He pictured a couple who had been married for decades. The wife sat knitting. The bloke sat in front of the fuzzy telly, watching the horse races, losing yet another bet—but nowhere near enough to deter him. He pictured the smell of smoke and beer. He pictured a happy, quiet life. A content life, where this couple were just happy to be in each other's company.

He pictured the lights going out, the couple going upstairs, and lying on the bed holding each other's hands and swallowing several pills together. Dying together.

He didn't know whether his version of events was accurate or true. He didn't know if that was how things had really gone down or not. But it was a story he could imagine. It was a possibility that didn't seem too ridiculous or too far-fetched. It was a familiar tale of tragedy in a world where tragedy had become the norm long ago.

"I'm sorry for pushing you earlier."

The voice came out of nowhere. To be honest, he drifted off into his own thoughts quite a lot. It wasn't a recent phenomenon. When you were used to living on your own, your inner voice kind of became your constant companion. For better or for worse.

But right now, Sam knew this wasn't his inner voice. This was the voice of someone he knew well.

He turned around and saw Seann standing there by the door.

Seann looked... genuinely remorseful; God fucking bless him. He was staring at the floor. Looked like a kid who'd stolen sweets from a shop, and Sam was the owner, pretending to be mortally pissed off with him when actually he was just mildly irritated.

Sam shrugged. "Leave it. Get some sleep."

"I just... I just worry sometimes that you're ignoring the truth right in front of us."

Oh. So that's how this shit was going to be, was it? Seann wasn't just here to apologise. He was here to further convince Sam he was in the wrong and to win him around to his way of thinking when really Sam couldn't think of anything worse. "Seann—"

"I'm not asking you to give up on Tara. I... I understand you can't just give up on someone you love like that. I get it more... more than you think."

Someone you love. Was it true? Did he love Tara? Fuck, probably. Why did he find the thought so... uncomfortable? When it was so clearly, well. *True*.

"Then what *are* you asking?"

Seann took a moment. He was silent. Like he was thinking really carefully about what Sam had said. Thinking really carefully about what he was going to say next.

And then he said something quite simple. Something quite clear.

"I just think you would get a lot of peace from accepting you can only do your best. That... that the only thing any of us can do, really, is our best. I think... I think you'd get a lot from accepting that."

Sam was silent. He didn't reply to Seann.

"And also... you shouldn't push other people away just because you're terrified of losing them."

Sam sat there. And as much as he'd braced himself to be thoroughly pissed off by what Seann said, he wasn't. He didn't feel pissed off. Not at all.

Instead, he felt... a weird kind of respect for Seann.

He'd stood up to him. He'd been honest with him. And in a weird way, he'd said something that kind of made *sense* to him.

He sat there, and he wanted to thank Seann for his words. He wanted to tell him he had a point. And he appreciated Seann speaking so frankly to him.

But then he swallowed a lump in his throat.

"Get some sleep," Sam said. "We go again tomorrow."

Seann opened his mouth. Looked like he was going to say something.

And then he closed his mouth, sighed, half-smiled, and nodded. "Goodnight, Sam," he said.

He walked out of the lounge, closing the door behind him and leaving Sam alone in the darkness.

Alone with his thoughts of tomorrow.

His thoughts of Tara.

And his thoughts of how he just couldn't let her go, no matter what.

"Wherever you are... if you're out there... I hope you're okay."

CHAPTER SIX

Kurt looked around at the remains of his empire and tried to process his emotions right now.

Sadness. Disbelief.

And rage.

He didn't know what time of day it was. It felt warm, and it seemed bright. He didn't know. Didn't have a fucking clue. It didn't matter, really, did it?

All that mattered were the people in front of him.

Or rather, the lack of people in front of him.

Something had happened. A breakout. People had got up, and they'd broken free. Some of them had died trying to escape. Others had killed his own people. There were bodies everywhere. Blood everywhere. Wounded people sitting against the walls. And he couldn't process how things had regressed so quickly. He couldn't understand how his home and his greatest life's work had fallen apart so drastically and so rapidly. He knew that woman, Tara, was responsible somehow. He knew she'd bumped off one of his people, then sneaked in here and set a load of people free. And credit to her, to be honest. She'd done what he would've done if he were in her shoes.

It wasn't Tara he was annoyed at. Not really. She'd just done her best to survive. In a way, he kind of admired that. In a morbid kind of way, it excited him.

No, it wasn't Tara he was annoyed at. Not really.

It was his own people for being so weak as to let this happen.

He looked around at them. Standing there. Lined up against the wall. Heads lowered. All looking so fucking weak and so fucking sheepish. Look at them. Pathetic. They were supposed to be alphas. They were supposed to be leaders. They were supposed to be strong.

But now... now, just looking at them made Kurt realise he was the only strong one here. They were only strong because of him. They weren't the leaders he wanted them to be. They weren't the strong people he wanted them to be. They were just... followers.

And, in a way, wasn't that what he'd wanted? Wasn't that how he'd wanted them to be, really? Because he knew what people were like when they got a sniff at power. He knew when people got too strong, they became jealous, envious, and they tried to bite off more than they could chew. He couldn't surround himself with people like that. He needed to surround himself with people who were strong but at the same time, weren't too strong.

But now, he started to question whether they had any strength about them at all.

"You let her escape," Kurt said. "All because you didn't control your goddamned urges for one fucking day."

One of the men whose name Kurt hadn't even bothered to memorise looked up and shook his head. "It—it wasn't us. It was—"

"I don't care who it was. What you did... what you did was complacent. The time we took to gather those people. The efforts we took rebuilding this place. And you just let it fall apart. You all just let it fall apart."

"We—we didn't!" another man gasped. Peter. Annoying-fucking-Peter. "We—we've always worked hard. We've—we've never slacked. You know that, man. But—but something just went wrong. And if—if that bitch hadn't broken free and started this, we wouldn't be saying this now."

Kurt looked around at Tara. She lay on the floor, unconscious. She was surrounded by blood. She didn't look in a good way.

And then he looked back at Peter. "Tara here did what any of us would've done if we were in her shoes. I admire her, in a way. The strength to do what she did. To cause what she caused. It took courage. And I can't take that away from her."

He looked at Tara again. Saw her lying there. Eyes closed. Wondering whether she was still even alive. Hoping she was, in a way. Because truth be told, he'd lost his passion for this place. He was only just realising that now, really. He'd built this empire. He'd created this prison. This sustainable source of meat and this sustainable source of women, who could maybe even form the future of this place.

But really, it was never about the meat. It was never about the sustainability. It was never about the community or the right way to survive.

Really, when Kurt looked at it clearly, he knew exactly what it was about.

It was about power.

His power.

Proving to himself that he was strong enough.

And he'd more than proven that.

So what now?

What came after you proved you were strong enough?

He looked at Tara, lying there, and the respect he felt for her, and the fire she awoke inside him, and he wondered... what if?

So he swallowed a lump in his throat. He took a deep breath. He looked out at these people—at his people—all lined up in front of him. These cowards. These weaklings. And really, he saw they were no different to the prisoners they trapped here, really. They were all in his prison. They were all just playing along with his game.

And somehow, that didn't satisfy him anymore.

He wanted more.

He looked ahead at each one of these people, and he felt a possibility opening up in front of him. Another option. Another way. A way of making things more challenging. A way of making things more exciting. A way of making things more… fresh.

He looked at them, then back at Tara, and he smiled and nodded. "You know… maybe I've been wrong. Maybe I've been harsh. And maybe you're right."

He walked over to Tara. He picked her up. And he dragged her over to the door while the rest of his people in here stared back at him. He could see the fear in their eyes. See the confusion in their eyes. See the panic and uncertainty.

"Boss?" one of them said. And it just wound Kurt up even more, in truth. Hearing them say 'boss' like they were some subservient little weakling… it just riled him up even more. Annoyed him even more. Was this how weak they really were? Had he been kidding himself for months? What made them any different from the people they'd kept as cattle when it really came down to it? And now the vast majority of those people were gone… what was their purpose at all?

"Don't worry," Kurt said. Smiling. "I'm going to deal with her appropriately. You… you all wait here. And you don't move. Understand? You don't move a muscle."

He glanced back at them. Back inside this warehouse. He looked at the reminders of the empire he'd built. He looked at the gaps where so many people had sat—people he'd gathered—and he felt a twinkle of pride. The best job he'd ever done. One he was so, so proud of. It felt good to be proud of a job he'd done. To look back and ask the question: could I have done any better? And to know, deeply, truly, that the answer was "no."

And then he looked at his people—the people who had let him down so dearly—and he knew it was the end of the road. He knew there was no going back. Not now the seed had been planted in his mind. The alternative had been glimpsed.

He walked out onto the corridor. Walked out of the main door. He lay Tara there in the sunlight. "You wait there," he muttered. "Although… I doubt you'll be going far."

And then he went back inside. Grabbed a rifle from the store room. One of the rifles he kept only for the most special of occasions. Only the most drastic of circumstances.

He walked back towards the main warehouse area, and he stood at that door.

Took a deep breath.

This was right.

This was what he had to do.

He opened the door, saw the gormless faces of his most devoted followers peer back at him. And then, as he lifted the rifle, he saw their panic and fear begin to grow.

"You should've run while you had the chance," Kurt said. "If you had any sense about you."

"Kurt, no!"

But by raising that rifle, he knew it was already too late. He knew that raising the rifle was an act of murder in itself.

So there was no going back now.

He took a deep breath.

And then he pulled the trigger, and he shot every one of them.

He shot them in the body. He shot them in the face. He shot them anywhere and everywhere, emptying the contents of his rifle all over them, watching their blood splatter all over the walls, watching them tumble over to their knees, watching them fall.

He watched them tumble all around him, and then as he was firing, he felt a part of himself die. A part, deep inside himself, completely disintegrate.

And he pictured Tara as he pulled that trigger—pictured her watching him through her bruised eyes—and he smiled.

He wasn't sure what he was going to do with her. Not yet.

But he knew he was going to do something. He knew she was going to play a part. In everything. A bigger part than perhaps he'd first even considered. A part that he still wasn't sure of the relevance of just yet. But a part he knew was significant.

He looked back at the blood all over his warehouse, and he took a deep breath of that putrid, fear-filled air, and his smile widened.

It might be the end of an era.

But it was the beginning of a new one.

CHAPTER SEVEN

Sam heard the noise outside and opened his eyes right away.

He was dreaming. Dreaming about Tara and Rebecca. Dreaming of them speaking. Smiling. Laughing. It was a nice dream. A dream he'd had before. Leonard was in it, as too were Marky and Harvey. And everything just felt so... calm. Everything just felt so safe. Safe in a way Sam hadn't felt in a long time. But... but there was something weird about this dream, too. There was something different this time. Something more unsettling than usual. They were in this safe place they usually were, with the sunshine, warmth, the sound of seagulls overhead, and the sea crashing against the shore. But also, there was... there was a smell in the air. A smell of burning. Of... of meat cooking over a barbecue. Only that meat wasn't appetising. It smelled... off-putting. It smelled sour. It reminded Sam of the smells in the warehouse. In Kurt's hellhole.

But then he opened his eyes.

It was dark. Still the middle of the night. He was still in the abandoned house. It was quiet in here. That old smell filled the air—the smell of cigarette smoke from long ago mixed with a strong floral perfume. He could hear a light breathing, which confused him and worried him for a second. When he looked around, he saw Seann lying there on the sofa, fast asleep. Weird. He wasn't in here earlier. He'd left this room. Sam must've dozed off, and he must've come back in here. Weirdo.

He lay there, and he listened to his heart beating through the silence. He'd heard something. He was sure of it. And he was pretty fucking sure it wasn't something in the dream, either. He'd heard movement. Movement in the house. Like... footsteps.

He got up. Crept to the door. Walked out of the living room and into the hallway, being careful not to disturb Seann. He didn't want to attract his attention. Seann spoke a lot, and these hours alone at night were pretty much the only time Sam got to himself at all these days. Couldn't even sleep in peace without the guy creeping back in here. Clearly had some sort of big attachment issues. Fuck, didn't everyone nowadays?

He walked out of the room and into the hallway. And he wondered whether maybe he *had* imagined this sound. He'd had auditory hallucinations before. Especially on that bridge between sleep and waking. Who was to say he hadn't imagined this sound again? And come to think of it, what *had* he even actually heard?

He needed to go back to the living room. He needed to get some sleep. If he was imagining hearing things, then he was clearly fucking exhausted. And he needed to be on his A game with all the tasks and challenges he had ahead.

He turned around and walked back towards the living room when he heard it.

Movement.

Something in the kitchen.

He stopped. Looked around, over his shoulder. His heart raced. He'd heard something. He'd heard some movement in the kitchen. And this time, it definitely wasn't a hallucination. He was sure of it.

He crept back into the living room slowly. Grabbed his rifle.

And then he crept back over the floor, over to the hallway, still doing everything he could not to wake Seann. Good job this guy wasn't responsible for keeping them safe. This bastard could sleep through a nuclear attack.

He walked out into the hallway and stared down towards the kitchen.

He could still hear that movement in there. That shuffling in there.

There was someone in there.

All kinds of thoughts filled his mind. All kinds of possibilities. A raider. One of Kurt's people. Or Kurt himself. Or...

Or Tara.

He thought about Tara. Imagined her in there, scavenging for food. He imagined the reunion. He imagined wrapping his arms around her. Pulling her close. He imagined the warmth, and he imagined the things he would say to her. The unspoken words he was finally, finally going to say to her.

He walked closer towards the kitchen. Right up to the door. He pushed it, just slightly, with his rifle.

And then he stepped inside it.

He saw the stacks of pots in the sink, flies buzzing around them. He saw the patches of water on the floor, specks of mould growing in those puddles. He saw the dinner table, plates laid, crumbs on there, which maggots feasted on. It didn't smell pleasant in here. It smelled... it smelled haunted. Like the ghosts of the people who used to live here still walked this house.

And then he heard the movement.

Over by the fridge.

There was a counter. A counter separating this side of the kitchen from the fridge area.

Someone was hiding behind that counter. There was someone in here.

He walked across the floor slowly. Held his rifle tight. He tried to figure out what to do. Should he speak? Or should he keep quiet? Had they heard him? No. If they'd heard him, they'd be dashing the fuck away.

He walked over to that counter. He could hear the shuffling even louder now. What the fuck were they doing?

He stood there. Rifle raised. Heart racing.

There was only one way to find out.

He jumped over the counter, and he saw it right away.

It wasn't a person. It was a cat. A small, skinny cat. It looked like it was stuck. Wedged in the cat flap. Trying to drag itself out of it.

Sam lowered his rifle. He sighed. He felt sad for the cat. But at the same time, he felt... disappointed, somehow. Because it didn't matter what noise it was, a part of him couldn't help hoping it might be Tara. No matter what. And no matter when.

He walked over to the cat flap. "Come on, you," he said. "Let's let you out of here."

The cat meowed at him as he lifted that flap. As it scurried off out into the wild. He didn't know where it was going. He didn't know what was going to happen to it. But it would find a way. It'd survived this far, and it would find a way to keep surviving.

Hopefully, like him.

And hopefully, like his people.

He crouched there by the cat flap when suddenly he heard something that made the hairs on the back of his neck stand right on end.

Footsteps.

Right behind him.

CHAPTER EIGHT

Sam heard the footsteps right behind him and knew he didn't have much time to react.

He spun around. Lifted his rifle. Went to pull the trigger and fire. Because someone was here. Someone was here, and they were sneaking up on him, and he was in danger, and—

"Sam! Jesus!"

Sam stopped. He was so close to pulling that trigger. But he managed to stop himself in a flash. Because that voice. He knew that voice well.

"Fucking hell, Seann," Sam said.

Seann stood there in front of him in the dark kitchen, shaking his head. "'Fucking hell' *me*? What about you? Pointing a frigging rifle at me?"

"You shouldn't be sneaking up on me like that."

"Sneaking *up* on you? I heard you walk out the room. Saw you grab your bloody rifle. Saw you walking down the hallway. I had to come see you were alright."

"You could've just asked."

Seann shook his head. "Sorry, mate. But I can't actually believe we're debating this right now. You pointed a frigging rifle at me in the dark. You almost—you almost frigging *shot* me. So get the hell off your moral high horse right now."

Sam shook his head. Wanker. Creeping after him in the night. He should know better than to make Sam jump.

"So why are you here, anyway?" Seann asked.

"It doesn't matter now," Sam said, standing.

"So let me get this straight. You come in here with a frigging rifle. You look like you're hunting a lion or something. And then when I come in here, you spin around, almost *shoot* me... and now you're saying it just doesn't matter?"

"It is what it is," Sam said.

Seann shook his head. He looked cornered. He often had this look on his face. He knew when to stop prying. When to stop pushing Sam. That was something this guy had in his favour, anyway.

But this time, something different happened.

This time, Seann didn't stop.

"I've had enough," Seann said.

Sam frowned. "You've had enough?"

"Yes. That's what I said. Exactly what I said."

"Had enough with—with what? With me?"

"I've had enough with all of it. I'm here to help you, Sam. I'm —I'm here because I want to help you. I could've walked away. I could've walked away with Rebecca and the others, but I didn't. I —I chose to join you. I could've made a different choice, but I chose to join you."

"Well, maybe you made the wrong choice," Sam muttered.

He kind of hoped Seann hadn't heard him the second he said it. It was just one of those... one of those brain farts, you know? Something you say but don't actually mean. Because Sam didn't mean to sound fucking ungrateful. He appreciated Sam's offer of help. But... but truth be told, he hadn't *asked* Seann to join him. So he couldn't exactly start acting like an arse right now about how Sam was being with him.

"What?" Seann said.

Which meant he'd heard Sam. He'd heard exactly what he'd said. Shit.

"Nothing," Sam said, shaking his head.

"No," Seann said. Raising his voice now in a way that Sam had never really heard from him before. "I'm not having that. I'm— I'm not having you shutting me down again."

"Shutting you down? This isn't a frigging relationship," Sam said.

"But we're supposed to be a frigging *team*," Seann said.

Sam couldn't help but smirk a little. "A 'team'?"

Seann flushed a bit. "Okay. Maybe that was a little embarrassing."

"Yeah. Yeah, it fucking was."

"Sam, don't be a dick," Seann said. "You know what I'm getting at. We've—we've been travelling for a month now. And I still feel like... Well, sometimes I feel like you'd rather I not be here at all."

Sam shook his head. "It's not that."

"Then what is it?" Seann said. "And—and is it something you think you'll be able to change?"

Sam stood there. He didn't want to be a dick. But he had to be honest with Seann. Could he change? Did he *want* to change?

He took a deep breath. And as he stood there, silent, Seann shook his head.

"The fact you even have to think about it says everything I need to know," he said.

Sam rolled his eyes. "What now?"

"I'm going," Seann said. "Tomorrow. I'll—I'll get out of your fucking hair if I'm that much of a problem. You ungrateful piece of shit."

"Hey. I never asked for your help." Sam knew full well he should keep his emotions in check, but at the same time, feeling unable to hold back.

"You're an ungrateful bastard," Seann said. "And if I stay here much longer… I just know you're going to end up shooting me anyway, one way or another."

"Might not be such a bad idea," Sam muttered.

"You aren't going to find her," Seann shouted. "No matter… no matter how much you convince yourself you'll find her, you aren't going to. She's gone, Sam. She's gone. It's already too late."

He looked into Seann's eyes. Saw how wide they were. He could see that expression on his face. Almost like there was a look of regret there.

And again, Sam knew he should keep his emotions under control. He knew he should keep his composure. He knew he should stay calm. Really, really calm.

But… sometimes, you just couldn't help yourself.

He threw himself at Seann.

Grabbed him.

And then he swung him around and threw him to the floor.

He lifted his finger. Pointed down at Seann as he lay there. "Don't you dare say that," Sam said. "Don't you dare."

Seann lay there. Blood trickling out of his nostrils. His eyes were wide. He looked afraid. And Sam didn't like that look. The way Seann was staring back up at him. Like he was a monster.

He wanted to apologise. He wanted to drag him back to his feet. He wanted to ask him if they could both forget this and move forward. But he knew there was no going back. He knew there was no erasing this moment from memory.

He went to turn around and run away when he saw something.

On the floor. Right beside Seann. He saw something.

And he didn't know what it was yet. He couldn't tell what it was. Not exactly.

But when he saw what it was—when he realised *exactly* what it was—it changed everything.

Everything.

CHAPTER NINE

Tara opened her eyes and knew she only had one opportunity to get away from this place.

So she had to take it.

And she had to take it now.

It was the middle of the night. Pitch black. It was quiet outside. Not windy, not rainy. So quiet and so still. She wasn't sure if that was a good or a bad thing. A good thing because it meant nothing was distracting Kurt, and no sounds risked waking him up. Or a bad thing because she knew it could be the sound of her own footsteps and movement that woke him up.

And she didn't want to wake him up. She really didn't want to wake him up.

Because if she woke him up... she dreaded to think what he might do to her.

She stared up into the darkness. She could hear him snoring beside her. She saw him, too. Eyes closed. A little smirk on his face. He had his arm around her. Not tight, but she knew any movement was a risk. Any movement risked waking him up. Disturbing him. He was a relatively light sleeper, in her experience. And that meant what she was planning was even more risky.

She had to be careful. She had to be so careful.

As she lay there in the dark, heart racing, the smell of his cologne lingering in her nostrils—fresh, aromatic, completely in contrast to his rotten core—she imagined she was with Jonno again. It felt like a lifetime ago. Lying beside him, feeling like she had to get away from him. Feeling like she had no choice but to run. But feeling... so trapped. Feeling like running was the least possible thing on the planet. Like she'd sleepwalked right into imprisonment.

But she'd done it. She'd done it, and she'd got away. And sure, her life hadn't exactly been *normal* since. Not in any way, shape or form. But she'd got away. She'd escaped that creep's clutches and seen him for who he really was. And she would get away from this prick, too. Because she wasn't some shrinking violet. Her fucking purpose in life wasn't to be captured. To end up some cunt's plaything.

Her purpose was much, much bigger than that.

She'd tried killing Kurt. She'd tried grabbing a knife in the night and stabbing him. She'd even thought about just trying to smother him in his sleep. And she'd thought about injecting him with some of that muscle relaxant he just loved to pump her with to keep her "agreeable", as he always joked. But he always kept that close. Always joked that there was no chance she was ever reaching his front right pocket—and if she did, she'd be gutted enough to discover it was the left pocket he kept it in. That was it. That was the weird joke of it all. But even so, he couldn't have much left now, surely?

But regardless, no matter what she tried, he always seemed to wake up. He always seemed to open his eyes at the worst possible moment. Almost like he was just playing with Tara. Like he was letting her get close to hurting him, then stopping her right when her hope was highest.

And that summed him up really, didn't it? He seemed to get a kick from giving people hope and then snatching it away right at the death. Like a predator.

But as she lay here right now, Kurt's sweaty arm around her, she knew she had to make a move. She knew it was now or never.

She sat up. Felt Kurt's arm sticking to her skin as she moved, clinging to her. She listened to him. Heard he was still snoring. He hadn't made a move. He hadn't noticed her. And that was good. It was good, but she needed to be swift. She needed to be quick.

She got up. Stood up. Walked right across the room. Over to the door. She knew where the floorboards creaked. She'd had enough days in this house to study where they were. She dodged them. Walked over them. And then she walked through the door without looking back and headed to the stairs.

She got to the stairs. Looked over her shoulder. She swore she could hear movement. She swore she could hear someone moving in the bedroom. Which meant—which meant he was awake. It meant he was awake, and he was coming for her.

And that meant she had no time at all.

She ran down the stairs, and suddenly, she lost her footing.

She slammed against the bottom step. Let out a little yelp that she couldn't hold back, couldn't suppress. And then as she lay there, totally still, listening to that silence, praying he hadn't heard... she heard something.

Footsteps.

She stood back up. Fear filling her body. She ran down to the bottom step, her ankle killing. She ran over to the front door and tried turning the handle. But it was locked. Fuck. He never locked this door. Never. It was like... it was like he could read her mind. It was like he knew she was planning on making a break for it tonight. How did he know? He couldn't read her mind. What signals had she given away that indicated she was going to make a break for it?

She started running to the kitchen when she heard the bedroom door open.

She froze. Like a rabbit in the headlights. She felt fear taking over her body. Fight or flight kicking in. She couldn't do this. She wasn't strong enough. She couldn't—

No.

She was strong.

And she was getting the fuck out of here.

She ran into the kitchen. Ran to the back door. Grabbed the handle as the footsteps banged against the stairs.

She went to turn the handle, and for a moment, for just a moment, she wondered what she would do if he'd done the fucking unthinkable—the thing he never did—and locked the door.

And then she noticed it.

The handle. It didn't turn. It was locked.

She stood there. Stood there as those footsteps got closer. As they powered down the stairs. And as she stood there, thinking about smashing a window, thinking about searching for the key, she knew she was running out of time. She knew there was already no time.

She saw a pad of paper on the kitchen table. A pen right beside it.

And even though she couldn't think exactly why she was doing it... it felt like her only hope right now.

She ran over to it. Grabbed that pen. And then she scribbled down onto that piece of paper the first thing she could think of as those footsteps crept closer.

She finished writing when she heard the door creak open.

She froze. Stared down at the table. Heart racing. Sweat trickling down her face. Because she knew he was here. She could feel his presence.

She dropped the pen. Put it down on the table. Looked at the desperate scrawl on the pad of paper. Wondered why she'd even bothered writing that note. Because it wasn't going to help. It was desperate. It was a last resort. It was the first thing that came to her. The only thing that seemed natural. And it wouldn't get her anywhere.

She turned around. Looked at the doorway. And she saw him standing there. Smiling at her. Wide-eyed. So tall. So pale. So slim. Smiling.

"Going somewhere?" Kurt asked.

CHAPTER TEN

Sam held the note in his hand and tried to wrap his head around exactly what he was looking at.

It was dark. Still the middle of the night. So it was hard to see properly. Hard to make out. He wondered if he was just tired. If maybe he was just completely exhausted and imagining things. It wouldn't be the first time. And it wasn't exactly unthinkable, either. He'd been through shitloads of different breeds of hell. It wasn't exactly unprecedented that he might fucking imagine something. Surely that was forgivable? Understandable?

But... but he didn't think he *was* imagining things.

He kept on reading this piece of paper, and he couldn't help wondering if maybe, just maybe, this was exactly what he thought it was.

He blinked a few times. Squinted even further into the darkness. He could hear Seann saying things to him. Hear him muttering things in the background. But Sam wasn't listening properly. He wasn't taking anything he said in.

He could only focus on this piece of paper. This pad he'd knocked onto the floor when he'd pushed Seann over in their shitty argument over nothing. This pad that had tumbled off the table and caught his eye right away.

He looked down on it, and he wondered... what if?

"Sam?"

He heard Seann. Looked up from the note. Saw him, blood trickling down his face from his nostrils. He saw a bruise forming around his eye. A little black eye. And he felt guilty about it. He shouldn't have snapped at Seann like that.

But somehow... somehow, that seemed irrelevant now. Somehow, it seemed like it didn't matter—as harsh and as ruthless as it sounded. The only thing that seemed to matter at this moment, at this instant, was the piece of paper. The note in his shaking hand.

"What is it?" Seann asked.

Sam looked at the note. Squinted right at it. And then he turned it around and held it out to Seann. "Can you see this?"

"Can I see what?"

"Don't fuck with me," Sam said. "The note. Can—can you see anything on there? Or is it all in my head?"

Seann studied the piece of paper. Looked really closely at it, squinting at it.

"Well?" Sam said.

Seann looked up at him. "I mean..."

"Do you see anything on there?"

"Obviously I see something on there."

"Writing?" Sam said.

"I mean, yeah. I see... I see writing. But—"

"You see it," Sam said. And he felt a wave of relief. He saw it. Which meant it was real. He wasn't imagining things. It wasn't all in his head after all.

"And do you see what it says?" Sam asked.

Seann shrugged. "Well, I can read."

"Well?"

Seann looked back down at the note. He looked like he was

really studying it. Really taking it in. Trying to wrap his head around what it said. And taking a damn long time about it in the process.

"You think it's her?" Seann asked.

Sam nodded. "The writing. I've—I've seen that writing before. Not often. But I've seen it. And... and it looks like hers."

Seann nodded. Looked back down at the note. It looked like his hands were shaking now.

"And if it is," Sam said.

"It changes things," Seann said.

"Yeah," Sam said. "Yeah, it does."

He looked at Seann. Seann looked back at him. He wanted to apologise to Seann for earlier. But at the same time, he wanted to grill him for telling him to give up on Tara.

Because this was evidence. This was evidence she was still out there. Right here, in Seann's hand.

He held out the note back to Sam. And when Sam took it, he looked at it again closely. Blinked a few times. Rubbed his eyes. Made sure he was right. Made sure he was absolutely certain.

And as he looked down at this note, he felt the hope rising inside his body. The first sign of hope he'd seen in so, so long.

The first sign that she was still out there. And she was close.

He read those words on the note again and again, and he felt a shiver creep down his spine.

Heading north. With him. Anyone finds this, NRS. That's where we're...

CHAPTER ELEVEN

Sam stood at the door to the house they'd spent last night in and stared out at the street, and he knew deep down that today was going to be very different.

It was morning. The sun was just rising over the horizon. Sometimes, when you stood there and stared out at this time of day, you could convince yourself the world was completely ordinary. That there was no blackout and that life hadn't changed a bit. Five a.m. was sleepy whether the power was on or not. For a few minutes, listening to the birds singing overhead, smelling that fresh morning air, you could really lose yourself in the idea that life was just exactly how it used to be.

But then, out of nowhere, you were snapped back into reality. You were always snapped back into reality.

And it was the note that snapped Sam back into reality.

He looked down at that note, sitting on top of that pad. He read those words scrawled on there again. *Heading north. With him. Anyone finds this, NRS. That's where we're...* That unfinished sentence, which trailed off into a scribble. And he could sense the desperation in those words. He could see how hurriedly they'd been jotted. He pictured the panic. The desperation with which they'd been written.

But... the very *fact* they had been written at all was something, wasn't it?

And the fact that he'd found it. Him, here, of all people. He didn't believe in signs. Didn't remotely believe in superstitious bullshit like that.

But this... this was enough to make him wonder if there were such a thing.

Heading north. With him.

A shiver crept up Sam's spine. Because he knew who the "him" was. And as unlikely as this seemed... it felt like she'd directed the note towards him. That in a moment of hopelessness, she'd written that note and prayed he'd find it. And by some miracle, he had found it. He was here. He was holding it. And he had an opportunity to act on it. A chance to do something about it.

Anyone finds this, NRS. That's where we're...

NRS. He didn't know what that meant. Was it a location? A group? An acronym for something Sam was forgetting? He really wasn't sure. Didn't have a fucking clue.

But it *was* something. And it was something more than he'd had yesterday, or the day before, or *any* day since losing her.

It was a trace of Tara. It was evidence she was still alive. Or at least that she *had* been alive, and she had been travelling north to some NRS, whatever or whoever that was. And that was fucking something.

Assuming it *was* Tara. No. He couldn't entertain the alternative possibility. It was clearly her writing. It had to be her.

He heard footsteps behind him. Turned around. Saw Seann standing there. His eye had bruised a bit after last night. Sam felt pretty bad for pushing him and snapping at him. But he hadn't brought it up. Neither of them had spoken about it. And the fact Seann was still here... well, that spoke for itself.

"How are we going to go about this?" Seann asked. No small

talk. No "good morning, how the fuck are you?" Just straight to the point. Which Sam appreciated. There was only one thing on both their minds. So there was no point beating about the bush.

Sam looked down at that note again. At her handwriting. He'd seen that writing before. A Christmas card she'd written for him back at Southfield. A birthday card, too. He was never one for cards or any kind of gesture that might peel back some of his layers and expose some of his vulnerability, really. But he remembered liking that gesture. He remembered saving that card. Treasuring it. Just like he treasured the Buzz Lightyear wing Leonard had given him before embarking on this so far fruitless journey.

He thought about Leonard. He hoped he was okay. He hoped they were all okay. And he hoped, one day, he'd see them again. With Tara by his side. Because if she *weren't* by his side... he'd always feel like he'd failed.

But then Sam remembered the immediate concern right now. The immediate goal.

"I guess there's only one thing we can do," Sam said.

"And what's that?"

Sam took a deep breath. The path ahead clearer than ever.

"We head north," he said. "We find Tara. And we make that bastard who abducted her pay for what he's done."

CHAPTER TWELVE

Tara walked down the road into the sunlight and got the feeling she was never getting away from Kurt.

It was morning. Nice morning by all accounts. Sunny. Warm. Pretty bright. She could see the buildings lined up either side of the road. All of them looked empty and abandoned. She kind of hoped they came across some group or other. Good or bad, she didn't really care. Just something that caused enough of a distraction so that she could get away from Kurt.

She listened to his footsteps hitting the road by her side and glanced around at him. Saw the knife he was holding. Saw the way he looked at her, that smirk rising up his face. She hated that he had this degree of control over her. She hated that even if she tried to run away, he'd find her. He'd hunt her down, and he'd find her. And if she *did* try to run away... he'd just make her life even more of a misery.

She thought about the note. The note she'd scrawled back at the house. She didn't even know what she'd written exactly. Only that whatever she *had* written was pretty desperate. What had she been hoping for? That Sam would find her, of all people? That wasn't going to happen. She didn't know where Sam was. She didn't know what'd happened to him. And one thing was for sure: Sam wasn't going to be out here, searching blindly for her. It just wasn't going to be the case.

But without hope... what did she have?

She thought back to the warehouse then. To what happened there. That day when everything changed. The day the uprising began. The day people decided enough was enough and made a break for it. The day she'd helped Rebecca escape. Helped Seann escape. Helped Marky escape.

And then she thought about... she thought about the position she'd found herself in. The way she'd stared death right in the face, and not for the first time.

And the way she'd stared *Dad* in the face, too.

She thought about Dad. Thought about the things he'd said to her. The things he'd told her. And then she thought about what happened, and...

No.

She didn't want to think about that.

She didn't want to think about the last time she'd seen him.

She didn't want to think about Kurt lifting that rifle. Firing at all his people. Firing at the prisoners that were left. And... and firing at Dad, too.

And she'd felt sad. Of course she'd felt sad when she witnessed him slumping onto his side, the blood trickling out of his lips. But at the same time... at the same time, she felt a sense of relief, too. Because he was suffering. He was in pain. He was on borrowed time with his cancer as it was. But now... now, he was gone. He was at peace, at last. Sad as it was, he was at peace.

And she wasn't sure why it was, but she felt like she'd been desensitised to loss, somehow. That she was growing worryingly used to the pain. And that was scary, wasn't it? That was really fucking terrifying. Especially when it was her own *dad* she'd witnessed die before her.

But at the same time... it felt like the end of an era. The last living person who knew the truth about Emily and what Tara had done was now gone. Was it wrong to say it was something of a relief? Was that really so awful? Of course it was fucking awful. But this world was awful. If anyone still alive claimed to have a completely clean conscience, they were either lying or deluded—and both were terrifying.

She looked around at Kurt. He was a... well, an *interesting* character for sure. She'd obviously made her mind up about this bastard. He'd murdered Millie right in front of her—right in front of everybody. He'd shown the absolute worst sadistic tendencies. And by all accounts, she was pretty sure he was the closest thing to a monster she'd ever come across.

And yet... since taking off however fucking long ago it was, Kurt hadn't laid a finger on her, sexually at least. He'd intimidated her, of course, psychologically and mentally. Sometimes, he'd even got a little physical. He'd made it perfectly clear she belonged to him, and that's the way it was going to be from now on. And sometimes... sometimes he seemed to suggest he was done with her. That he was going to get rid of her. Bump her off. She got that feeling she was very much disposable to him. She didn't know why he kept her around. Whether it was to punish her. Or whether it was something far, far deeper than that.

But there was something. Something in the way he looked at her when he didn't think she noticed. Like he was weighing her up somehow. For what? She wasn't sure. Trying to get the measure of her? Or like a snake, eyeing up its prey before indulging in it? Tara once heard a story about a pet snake who used to lie beside its owner's daughter, full length. Owner thought it was cute. Daughter was completely comfortable with it. One day, the owner got home and found her daughter's ankles sticking out of the snake's mouth. As she sliced away at the snake's solid muscles, desperately trying to rescue her daughter, it dawned on her that the snake wasn't lying beside her for comfort. It was lying beside her to measure her up.

Maybe Kurt was just like that snake.

Or maybe Tara was that snake to Kurt.

Time would tell.

"Where are we going?" Tara asked.

Kurt looked around. He always looked surprised to hear Tara speak of her own accord. It was like it wasn't in his plan, somehow. Something he hadn't prepared for. "You're going where I go," he said.

"I know that," Tara said. "But I mean, if I'm going where you go, can't you be a little more specific?"

"You know where we're going."

"This 'NRS' group," Tara said. "If that's what we've decided they are."

Kurt nodded. "Right."

Tara remembered the first time she'd seen the sign for the NRS. The announcement that they were close by. The decision between them that it had to be some kind of group. An arrow pointing north and a note beneath with all kinds of details. Details about this community. Details about how many people were there. And details about the sorts of people they were looking for. A large group. Searching for any physically or mentally capable enough to help out. Which sounded ideal. That was the sort of community anyone still alive was looking for nowadays, right?

And she felt torn. Because, of course, she wanted to get to a stable community. She wanted to find somewhere safe. That was the dream at the end of the day, wasn't it?

And yet... she didn't want to go anywhere with Kurt. Because Kurt was like poison. She feared he'd find a way to claw his way into someplace good. Find a way to work to take down the people that ran that place. Or even just cause some mayhem. Enough mayhem to just... well, fuck with things for a bit. Because she wasn't exactly sure what his motive was. What he was looking for in life. Just that he wanted to cause chaos.

"And when we get there," Tara said. "What then?"

"What?"

"We get to this place," Tara said. "And we're supposed to just go in there and play happy families? Act like a married couple?"

Kurt shrugged. "I can think of worse ideas."

"And you expect me to just play along?"

Kurt looked at her. Smiled. "I'd say it's in your best interests to do exactly as I say, Tara. I thought we'd already established that?"

Tara shook her head. Rolled her eyes. "You act like you're the first man to take ownership of me in my life. Trust me. I've been there. More times than I'd like to admit."

Kurt's eyes narrowed a bit. This often happened. Like he was really studying her. Trying to get a read on her. Struggling to understand her. She probably didn't play into the terrified damsel role he was used to. Did that intrigue him? Probably. And in a way... in a way, that was a good thing. Because if intriguing this man kept her alive a little longer, that gave her more of a chance to escape him. And more of a chance to make him pay.

"Truth be told," Kurt said. "I haven't fully decided what my intentions are yet. I've... I've had an empire. I watched that empire fall. And now... I don't know. I kind of like the life on the road. I kind of like taking the back seat. Maybe... maybe leadership isn't for me, after all."

She listened to these words coming out of this man's mouth, and she figured he was the oddest person she'd ever met. The oddest fucking person she'd ever come across. Because his words. The things he said. They just didn't have a ring of truth to them. It was like he was performing. Like this was all a performance—his entire persona was a performance—and if you scratched away at the surface and kept on going, you'd find nothing but a deep, dark, evil void hiding inside.

"Maybe we'll reach that place," Kurt said. "Maybe you'll grow to like me. Grow to realise I'm just a man doing the things he has to do to survive. I'm a man who tried something different. Something—something successful, may I add. And really... we're not so different. Not at our core."

Tara looked into Kurt's eyes. Deep into his eyes. Got real close to him. So close that he could punch her or stab her if he really wanted to.

"You'll never have a fresh start," Tara said. "Never. I'll never let you have a fresh start. Because you don't get to have a fresh start. Not after the things you've done. Not with the things you're responsible for. You don't get to just decide whether you get a fresh start or not."

Kurt's smile faltered just for a second.

"I'll kill you," Tara said. "Before you have a chance at a fresh start, I'll kill you. That's a promise. And it's a promise I intend to keep."

For a second, for just a second, his smile fell away entirely. And for that second, Tara realised who she was looking at. She realised she was looking at Kurt's true face. That this was the void hiding underneath when you scratched away at the surface completely. And it was angry, lost, and afraid.

And then he forced a smile again.

"You think you're in control," he said, pulling her so close she could smell his sour breath mixed with his sickeningly fresh cologne. "You think you are calling the shots. You think there's a nice Hollywood ending to all this. But there isn't. There isn't. Not unless... not unless you learn to start playing nicely."

And then he pressed the knife to her chest.

"Because *I'm* the man with the knife. And I'm the man who hasn't quite decided what I want to do with you. Not yet."

He pushed the knife in further. Pushed it so hard she swore she felt her skin splitting.

"But for now..."

He pulled the knife away. Lowered it. And then he patted her on the back and nudged her forward.

"For now, you walk. We both walk."

Tara didn't want to do what this man told her to do. She was sick of doing what narcissistic control freaks told her to do.

But right now, standing there, that knife still pointed at her... it depressed Tara to admit that she didn't have a choice.

She looked at his coat. At the bulge where he kept that muscle relaxant syringe in his pocket, close to him at all times.

She took a deep breath. Swallowed a lump in her throat.

And then, as much as it pained her, Tara walked.

She thought about that note.

She thought about Sam.

And as much as she hated being reliant and dependent on others... Tara prayed.

CHAPTER THIRTEEN

Sam walked down the road into the light and held Tara's note tight in his hand.

He and Seann were heading north. It was warm and bright. The streets looked like every other street—like the remains of a war zone, falling completely to shit. It was quiet. He could hear birds singing, and he could hear the occasional barking of dogs in the distance, but other than that, nothing but silence. The air smelled vaguely of smoke. He could taste something in his mouth. Something like... something like blood.

He felt the sharp stump from the tooth that had snapped away in his mouth a matter of weeks ago. It was easy to forget he'd been a prisoner so recently. Tied up, trapped in a living hell. That sort of shit was bound to take a toll, mentally and physically. There was bound to be trauma for years from that experience.

But he hadn't had time to think about the trauma. He hadn't given himself a chance to mope about it or anything like that. Or about the fact that he felt like passing out with every single footstep he took. He was exhausted. Completely broken. But he'd kept himself busy. Kept himself focused. Kept himself distracted.

Maybe when he finally found what he wanted, he'd drop dead with the exhaustion of it all right on the spot.

But it was when he took some downtime that it came back to him. The blindfold. The sound of screaming. The smell of shit and vomit and raw meat in his nostrils...

It all combined with the rest of his trauma from the past in an awful, sickening concoction.

"So where actually are we going?" Seann asked.

Sam rolled his eyes. He was kind of torn about Seann. On the one hand, he felt guilty for snapping at him last night. He could still see a reminder of what he'd done with that bruise under his right eye, where he'd slammed against the floor when he'd shoved him over. But on the other hand... Seann *was* kind of annoying. That's something he'd come to realise in the time he'd spent with him. He spoke too much. Asked too many questions. And that didn't gel with Sam's personality all that much.

And now here he was. Asking another stupid fucking question.

"North," Sam said.

"Be less specific, why don't you?"

"The NRS. That's where we're going."

"Ah, yes. The vague NRS. We don't know whether they're a group or whether it's a place. But that's where we're heading."

"You didn't have much of a problem with this when we found the note," Sam said.

"I've had time to think about it since then."

"Maybe that's your problem. Too much thinking about shit."

"What if it's dangerous?" Seann asked.

Sam shrugged. "It might well be."

"And still we're walking right toward that place. Because we're reckless. And that's just who we are and what we do."

"Couldn't have said it better myself," Sam said.

Seann shook his head. And Sam knew he should leave him. He

should leave him to sulk and roll his eyes. Because he was still here. Even if he had reservations, he was still here, and he was still walking with Sam. So he couldn't have *that* much of a problem with it all, right?

But Sam wasn't in the mood for letting things drop. "What's your problem?"

Seann sighed. "I just don't understand why we can't show a few more... precautions. That's all."

"The time for precautions is over," Sam said.

"Very bold. Very macho. But exactly the kind of philosophy that will get you killed. And me, too."

"I..." He stopped himself from snapping. From saying something else he didn't want to. And this time, for a change, he did something he wasn't expecting to do. He... he allowed himself to be *honest*.

"I failed Tara," Sam said. "And I can't... I can't give up on her. Especially not now there's a chance. Especially not now there's hope."

Seann was silent for a second. Like that moment of honesty had floored him too.

And then he walked over to Sam. Put a hand on his back. Patted him like he was a sad dog or something.

"You didn't fail Tara," Seann said. "You're still here. You're still searching for her. Right?"

Sam shook his head. And he felt it. He felt those words resonating deep inside him. The truth, buried deep inside, deep beneath his standoffish-ness and his obsession with finding Tara. His fear. His fear of losing people. That same fear forcing a distance between him and Seann. Making him reluctant to even *want* to get to know him.

"If you want to go your own way," Sam said, lowering his head, heart racing, "I understand it. I—I get it. I've been a bit of a cunt."

He glanced back up at Seann. Saw him shaking his head. "I'm

not going anywhere, buddy. I'm in this. Just like you. Frodo and Bilbo. Only less…"

"Gay?" Sam said.

Seann shrugged. "Debatable."

Sam smiled at Seann. Seann smiled back, laughing a little. And then Sam turned around to the road ahead. He didn't know how far north they were going to go. He didn't know how long he would be walking. He didn't know what he was going to find, what the NRS was, or anything like that.

But where Tara was concerned, he was never going to give up.

He went to take a step through these sun-drenched streets when suddenly something caught his eye.

"Seann," Sam said.

"What?"

"Look."

Seann walked up to him. Squinted up ahead. "What?"

And Sam wondered whether he was hallucinating for a second. Whether this was a figment of his exhausted, obsessed imagination.

"Oh," Seann said.

Sam looked around at Seann. Saw him staring ahead, wide-eyed. Partly excited. And partly afraid. Exactly how Sam felt.

"Well," Sam said. "I'd say this is a good sign, wouldn't you?"

Seann quite visibly swallowed a lump in his throat. "Good," he said. "Or bad. But it's definitely a *sign*. That's for sure."

Sam turned around. He looked ahead at what he'd seen.

Whether it was good or whether it was bad, one thing was for certain.

It *was* a sign. Literally.

But it was what was written on that sign that really caught his attention.

Those letters. Those three letters that stopped him dead in his tracks.

NRS.

―――――

CHAPTER FOURTEEN

―――――

Sam saw the sign up ahead, and he knew it was a turning point. He just still wasn't so sure exactly what it meant.

The sign was an old road sign. A brown one. Tourist attractions listed on it. A castle. A zoo. An aquarium. An arena.

But sprayed over the top of it in white paint, those three unmistakable letters.

NRS.

And then, right by the side of those letters, an arrow pointing ahead. Pointing north.

Sam stood there. Heart racing. Taking it all in. It just looked like standard graffiti. The sort that Sam would've ignored if he hadn't seen it written on Tara's note.

"I think it looks kind of..." Seann started.

"Go on."

"Well, you're going to hate me for saying this. But I think it looks kind of—"

"Creepy?" Sam said.

Seann nodded. "I was going to say 'ominous'. But yeah. It's nice to be kind of on the same page as you for a change."

Sam looked back around at the sign. Seann was right. It was ominous. And it was creepy. And it felt kind of refreshing to be honest to himself about that without letting the Tara links blind him. And if he ran into it without any mention of it on that note from Tara, what would he have thought? Well, he would almost definitely have turned the fuck around and made damned sure he didn't go in the direction it was pointing.

But at the same time... that note. Tara's note. That's where she was going. That's where she was heading. That's where she might already be. So he couldn't let any hunches or fear distract him from the task at hand. He knew he was being blinded a bit by the note. And he knew it was a gamble. He knew it was a risk. The sort of risk he wouldn't be keen on taking, usually.

But... well, this was a special case. This was different. Never underestimate the power emotion had to sway you towards even the most dangerous of situations.

"What are we thinking?" Seann asked.

Sam gulped. His throat was dry. He was nervous. Hated to admit it, but he was. Nervous about being honest with Seann, too. "I... I think it's creepy. And ominous. And I don't like it."

"I sense there's a 'but' coming..."

"But... Tara's heading that way. So I... I don't see that we have another choice."

Seann stood there. Sam fully expected him to disagree. To tell him to get stuffed. To tell him they absolutely were not heading in this direction because it was dangerous, and it was too much of a risk, and all that crap.

"We need to be careful," Seann said.

Which was... far milder than Sam was expecting. He wasn't really protesting or objecting. That felt like progress. And in a way... well, Seann had a point, didn't he? They did need to be care-ful. They did need to watch themselves. They couldn't be too reckless. Because if something happened to them, then what hope was there for Tara?

"You're right," Sam said.

"Wow."

"What?"

"For a second there, I thought I heard you say I was right. Not sure if I imagined it, though."

"Fuck off."

"There we go. That's more like it."

Sam looked back at that sign. He saw the grey clouds in the sky gathering overhead. Similarly fucking ominous. He hoped it wasn't a sign. A sign of trouble in the distance. Weirdly enough, as superstitious as it sounded, the weather had been a weirdly accurate predictor of events since the world went to shit. Reality really did imitate fiction, sometimes.

"I wonder if... if Rebecca and the others have found this place?"

He thought about Rebecca. About Leonard, Harvey, Marky, and Claude. He didn't know where they were. He didn't know if they were safe. He didn't know whether they'd found anywhere at all.

But he had to believe they had. Because thinking about the alternative... that brought even more pain to his chest. Especially since he'd been so focused on finding Tara that he'd forced them to the back of his mind.

He took a deep breath. They would be okay. They *had* to be okay.

"Come on," Sam said. "No point standing around."

Seann looked at him. Opened his mouth. For a moment, he looked like he was going to argue. To protest.

But then he just closed his mouth, nodded, and sighed.

"Right," he said.

Sam looked back up at that sign. At the letters, NRS, whatever they meant. And then at the arrow pointing into the distance.

And then, he took a deep breath, and he walked.

Overhead, the clouds thickened even more, and rain began to fall...

CHAPTER FIFTEEN

Gerald Leach had spent plenty of days since the power went out wondering whether today might be his last. But today, more so than ever, he was pretty certain that if he didn't get things under control before sundown, it really was the end of the road for him.

It was morning. Thankfully. Which meant he had plenty of time to work with. The day started off nice, but it seemed to be getting cloudier. Cooler. The transition phase between summer and autumn. He never liked this time of year. Always reminded him of childhood. The end of the summer holidays. Returning to school for another year—a year that felt like eternity. A year that felt like hell.

He never enjoyed school. People took the piss out of him. Mostly for his name. He wasn't sure why. Well, he was, in a way. He figured Gerald wasn't exactly a cool name like some of the others. It was kind of an entry point to getting under his skin. A way of people finding a weakness in him. And once they figured that was a weakness... well, you know how it is. Kids can be relentless.

The bullying was rough. Every day, he'd wake up, throw up,

have a breakdown, panic attack, and pray his mum didn't send him to school. Dad would slap him. Tell him to shut the fuck up. And no matter how much he argued or protested, he'd always end up in school. He'd always end up walking down that path hoping today was the day they moved on to someone different. And then something would happen to destroy his hope. All his hope. Someone would trip him up. Someone would call him a rude name. Someone would spit chewing gum into his hair. And the vicious cycle would repeat all over again.

He felt that same nervousness now as he stood there in the old cafe just off the main road in town. They'd been living here for a while. They had a few supplies—shit they'd stolen from passers-by and stuff they'd been given by the groups they kidnapped for. But supplies were running thin. Very thin. And his people weren't happy about it. He knew this place was good. He knew this place was safe. And he didn't want to just walk away from it. He didn't want to turn his back on it. He didn't want to leave it. At the end of the day, it was home, and nobody liked moving home. But it was starting to feel like he didn't have much choice.

"We can't keep surviving on no food," Carlton said. Carlton was a loudmouth. He always thought he had the right idea about how to do things, but really he was clueless. He definitely had his eye on leadership of this small group, now standing at eleven. A group that, somehow, Gerald had ended up leading. They met at a community out west a few months ago. The first place Gerald felt like he'd fit in his entire life. And then, when that community fell... they left that place together. Forged an alliance of their own.

They'd done some bad things. They'd stolen from people. They'd taken control of a few roads. They'd made people pay tolls for passing through. They'd demanded people handed over their supplies as payment. They'd sold people into slavery—one of the more fruitful business endeavours. Sometimes, they'd killed people when they hadn't played ball.

And Gerald felt guilty about it. Of course, he felt guilty about it. What decent person *wouldn't* feel guilty about doing the things he'd had to do?

But this was the new world. This was just survival now. You had to adapt, and you had to become the leader, or you died. It really was as simple as that.

But recently, the roads through town here had grown quiet. All of their hot spots for "demanding payments" from passers-by had gone quiet. It was like people had caught wind that this was a toll road, so were avoiding it. Finding other ways of getting where they needed to go. And that was bullshit. Not *just* because it meant Gerald's group was low on supplies. But also 'cause they had deals with other groups like theirs. Supply and demand type deals. They got these other groups what they needed, and they provided for them in turn. Some weird bunch down south had a big industrial site and always wanted Gerald to grab people for them—the plumper, the better, whatever the fuck that meant.

And Gerald did. No questions asked. 'Cause that group supplied them with food in turn. Meat. Real good meat. Succulent. Juicy. Tender.

He never thought to ask what that meat was. Whatever it was, it was delicious.

Maybe he was better off not knowing what it was.

But now that place had gone quiet, too. As much as he hadn't been expecting it, it'd gone the way of every other group—the way every group ended up.

They were running on reserves, and they were almost all out.

"Then what do you suggest?" Gerald said.

"We move on from this place. Fuck all people come through here anymore."

Stacey nodded. "I think he's right."

"And move where?" Gerald said.

"Anywhere!" Carlton said. "Anywhere is better than here. Anywhere with—with people. Anywhere with prospects. God forbid we might actually have to *take* somewhere for ourselves rather than just waiting for people to stumble by here."

"Oh, the eleven of us?" Gerald said. "With no guns? We just stumble into a community and ask them to hand their shit over? Because that worked so well with the NRS, didn't it?"

"Don't talk to me about the NRS."

"No. *You* need to remember. We lost people. Good people. Because we tried to do shit your way. And that's why we can't do things your way. Not anymore. That's why... thats' why we have to be patient."

Carlton was silent. Stacey was silent. The rest of his people, all sitting around in here looking various degrees of pissed off, were all silent.

"We stick together," Gerald said. "We wait. Just a little longer. We—we have faith in this place. Because it's served us well so far. We—we come up with a proper plan. A proper backup plan. All of us. Together. But... but running away from this place is not a plan conducive to survival right now. Running away from this place is suicide. You all know it. So let's not turn on each other. Let's work together. Not against each other. Okay?"

Gerald looked at his people, at all his people. When he glanced at every one of them, he noticed they turned away. They looked down at their feet. Or they looked out the window. None of them wanted to hold eye contact with him. None of them.

And as he looked back at Carlton... he knew he was running out of time. He knew life was ruthless now. He knew that if they didn't find any supplies soon—or any people they could use for bartering or something—then his time was up. They would turn on him. They would kill him in his sleep. And he wasn't ready to go. Not yet.

He stood there in the cafe in front of all his people. And he made a bargain he wasn't sure he could make. "One more day," he said. "That's all I ask. One more day. And then... and then if we find nobody or nothing... we move on. We try somewhere else. We try something else. Okay?"

Nobody said a word. And the lack of protestation, Gerald had to take as a bonus. He had to take as a plus.

He looked out the window. Outside at the grey skies. At the rain falling down. And he looked down the road, right down towards that nearby road sign with NRS etched over it in graffiti.

He didn't believe in God.

But right now, Gerald Leach found himself praying for a goddamned miracle.

CHAPTER SIXTEEN

Sam walked down the street and couldn't shake the feeling he was being watched.

It was late morning. Felt like he'd been walking for days. Figured he had, in a way. He and Seann hadn't really stopped ever since they'd left the group and gone searching for Tara. The odd hunting break. The odd cooking break. But otherwise, there hadn't been much time for downtime. Because how the fuck could you take any downtime when time itself was of the essence?

But the more days passed, the more Sam started to lose hope. He didn't want to admit it. Not even to himself. But he knew how it was when someone went missing. Not even just since the blackout. Before then, too. It's not like the movies or the TV shows. When someone goes missing, if they aren't found within the first couple of days, then there's a good chance they're never gonna be found.

But then he thought of all the evidence he'd had to the contrary. Finding Rebecca again. Finding Claude again. Finding Leonard again.

Hell, he'd been lucky. An absurd level of luck. Maybe this time, his luck was finally going to run out.

The streets were quiet and empty. They never got any less creepy. High streets, devoid of life. Kind of reminded him of lockdown. He'd gone out for a walk through town because fuck the government telling him what he could and couldn't do while partying the fuck away behind closed doors. And he was amazed to see how quiet it was. There was an edge, almost. A lot of druggies and homeless about, and a fair few rough kids too. And it felt like the atmosphere might just turn at any given moment.

But this... this was like that but on steroids. Because the people *were* gone. They weren't just hiding away indoors: they were, for the most part, dead. The druggies had overdosed. The homeless were dead. And the kids... well, they were almost certainly dead, too.

The only people left now were the ones who'd been strong enough to make it this far.

Or ruthless enough.

And that was a scary frigging thought.

He could see the arena in the distance. A gig venue he'd been to before. And he couldn't shake the feeling they were getting closer to it. That those signs were leading *right* towards it. And he wasn't sure how he felt about that.

"So how will we know?" Seann asked.

Sam looked around. Shit. This guy wasn't quiet often, but when he *was,* it was an absolute treat. "Huh?"

"This NRS. The sign. The arrow ahead. How will we know when we've found the place? Or the people. Or whatever the fuck 'NRS' is."

Sam sighed. "I mean, if it's worth signposting, then I'd say there's a good chance we'll see it, don't you?"

"And what if we get there—assuming it's a place. What if we get there, and Tara isn't there?"

Sam shook his head. "Keep walking."

"It's a legit concern, though, right? What if we get there, and she's not there? Or—or if someone else wrote this as a trap? Or if the NRS aren't so welcoming? Or if we get there and Rebecca and the others are there but she's not—"

"Then I keep searching," Sam said. "I... I'm not losing her. I'll keep going. Until I find her. Because—because that's what I have to do."

Seann looked right at him. Nodded. But he had this almost sympathetic look on his face. Like he was a doctor delivering news of a terminal illness to a kid.

"What's that look?"

"What's *what* look?"

"Don't bullshit me," Sam said. "You know the look I mean."

Seann opened his mouth like he was going to protest. And then he just sighed. "I just... One thing I've learned in life—"

"Oh, here we go."

"What?"

"One of your little speeches."

"My little speeches? What's that supposed to mean?"

"Trust me. You know exactly what it means."

"I don't know whether to be offended or flattered. But... but all I wanted to say was... well, life's completely out of control, Sam. It's—it's out of our hands. We can only control what we can control. Ourselves. Our—our own actions. We can only do our best. We can only ever do our best. And doing our best... well, that's not failure. Sometimes... sometimes life just has different ideas about shit."

Sam looked at him. Felt a little uncomfortable. He could see from the way Seann was talking that this wasn't just about Sam. It was about something he'd been through. Something he'd experienced. Something he'd never spoken about.

And then, before Sam could ask him what he was talking about, he walked on, up ahead.

Sam watched him walk on. It was interesting seeing a vulnerability to Seann that he didn't previously know was there. But as they walked, as much as this guy annoyed Sam, it suddenly struck him how little he knew about him. How little he knew about his past.

He wanted to ask him more questions about himself when suddenly he saw something right up ahead.

He stopped. Seann stopped. Both of them stood there. Staring up at the street lamps above.

"Shit," Seann said.

Sam swallowed a lump in his throat.

"Should we... should we turn back? Or find another way?"

Sam looked ahead. At the street. It looked empty. It looked abandoned. And as much as he knew he needed to be careful—they both needed to be careful—he thought about that NRS sign, how time was of the essence, and how this was the most direct route, so whether he liked it or not, he had to take it. He didn't have another choice.

"Come on," Sam said, tightening his grip around his rifle. "But be on your guard. I don't like this."

Seann shook his head. Clearly wasn't happy about this.

"I hope you're making the right call here, Sam," he said.

Sam nodded. "Me too."

And then they walked.

Above them, surrounded by clouds of flies, dead bodies dangled from the street lamps.

CHAPTER SEVENTEEN

Sam walked through the abandoned town and couldn't stop thinking about the dead bodies hanging from the street lamps.

It was the smell that stuck with him. He hadn't noticed it at first. Probably because the wind wasn't blowing all that heavily. But as he walked underneath them, that sour stench filled his nostrils. A smell he found all too familiar. A smell he'd almost grown used to when he was locked up in Kurt's place. Almost. Because you could never fully get used to that smell. And if you did... well, something was seriously wrong with you.

The clouds were back. There'd been a sunny stretch a little while back when they found the bodies hanging from the lampposts. Flies buzzing around them, their sound filling his ears. But now it was cloudy again. There was a breeze picking up. He could hear old doors creaking. Wind chimes. And every little movement caught his eye. Every single little movement captured his attention. He was on guard. Well alert. Because he got the feeling some of those bodies weren't all that old. Which meant someone had been here recently. Someone had propped them up there. A warning? He wasn't sure.

But there was one thing for sure.

"What if it's this NRS lot who did it?"

When Seann said those words, he kind of spoke Sam's thoughts and fears into existence. He didn't want to admit that's what he was thinking about or worried about. But he was bound to be. Something was off here. Those NRS signs had pointed this way. They'd pointed right to this place. What if the people who had done this were the NRS—if they were a group? What if those signs were a trap? And what was to say Tara's note meant *anything*, really? Maybe Kurt knew the NRS people. Maybe he knew them, and they were just as savage as he was, and that's why he was taking Tara there.

Or maybe it wasn't even Tara's note at all...

No. He couldn't think like that.

He wasn't sure about anything. Didn't have a fucking clue, in all truth.

But the only thing Sam was sure about was that they needed to search this place. Because if there was a chance Tara had been here... he couldn't just let that pass.

"We need to search the place properly," Sam said.

"I'd rather just keep walking. But I can understand your concern."

Sam swallowed a lump in his throat. Past the abandoned buildings, he could see the arena. The old gig venue where tons of bands used to come into town and play. He could see old posters falling apart on the brick wall. The 1975. Ariana Grande. Memories of the past. He wondered where those people were now. Whether they were still out there. Whether they were still even alive. Because fame didn't buy you anything. When the power went out... you were just as valuable as everyone else.

Or value-less.

They kept on walking through the streets. Constantly alert. Constantly looking from side to side. They checked a few old stores, but they were empty. Abandoned long ago, by the looks of things.

It was only when they got closer to the arena that something caught Sam's eye.

"There," Sam said, raising a hand and pointing.

"What?"

"NRS," Sam said. "The sign."

"Shit."

There was an NRS sign on the side of the arena wall. More of that white graffiti. And it was pointing right down an opening that led inside the arena.

"You sure about this?" Seann asked.

"If it says NRS, then Tara might be there."

"But—but walking into an arena. Into an enclosed space. That... that doesn't sound such a wise idea to me."

And Sam heard him. He heard his concerns. He really did. They were the sorts of concerns he would have himself if he was on the outside right now.

But he wasn't on the outside. He was on the inside. And Tara was out there. She said on the note they were heading north, towards the NRS. So any single trace of the NRS needed investigating.

"Sam," Seann said. "Remember what I said. About... about trying."

Sam narrowed his eyes. "If there's a chance she's in there... I won't just walk by. I can't. Or it's all been for nothing. I... I need to search this place. With or without you."

And then he turned around, and he walked towards the arena.

But as he walked towards that arena, he couldn't shake that instinctive feeling he was making a terrible mistake.

CHAPTER EIGHTEEN

Gerald Leach had no idea how long he'd been walking when he finally saw a sign of hope right in front of him.

First, he'd seen the bodies. The bodies dangling from the street lamps. And they'd given him the creeps. Made him want to go right back home. Because—because it just further confirmed his suspicions that this was a terrible idea. That they shouldn't have come out here at all. That they should've stayed far, far away from here and had a little more patience back home.

But now they were here, standing in the middle of this road outside the arena, and he saw the two people—the two men—with their rifles and their rucksacks, presumably filled with supplies, and he started to wonder if maybe—just maybe—this might not have been such a terrible idea after all.

He looked around at Carlton. Saw him staring at him. Smiling. "Well," he said. "Looks like we might be in luck."

Gerald turned around to that arena entrance, took a deep breath, and swallowed a lump in his throat.

Maybe they *were* in luck after all.

CHAPTER NINETEEN

Sam stepped into the arena, and for a moment, he felt like he was back in the old world again.

The arena was so echoey. The seats were all empty. The floor was covered in dust. A few plastic cups were lying on their sides by his feet. The stage was curtained and covered. And even though this place had clearly been occupied since the last gig in here, there was still that smell to the air. That faint hint of weed that always clung to the walls of gig venues like this. The slight stickiness to the floors where tons of booze had been chucked.

He looked up at the stage, and he thought back to when he and Rebecca came watching Kings of Leon here years ago. Standing right by the front. Rebecca, who had a history of attending gigs and a keen interest in music, telling him they would be fine up top. That there was no place to experience a gig other than the front. And Sam, well. He was sceptical. She'd been trying to convince him to go to a gig with her for years. But it just wasn't his thing.

He'd bought her tickets for her birthday with a friend. Only her friends couldn't make it, and Rebecca wasn't too keen on going on her own.

So who was the white knight who stepped in and saved the day? Yeah. You guessed it.

It was fine at first. People weren't rammed too close together. A few arseholes throwing booze and shoving, that kind of thing. But then the place got more and more packed, and Sam grew more constricted, more claustrophobic. And as he stood there in the heat, surrounded by all these bodies, he found himself back in Iraq. He found himself standing there, rifle in hand, the body of Yannis in front of him. Lying flat in a pool of blood.

His heart picked up. He couldn't breathe properly without thinking about it. He tried to swallow a lump in his throat, but he couldn't even swallow.

And he was surrounded. Surrounded by a bunch of numpties shouting something about sex being on fire. And he just wanted to get the fuck out of that place.

So he'd walked. He'd walked, and he'd pushed, and he'd shoved his way out of that crowd. He got spat on as he shoved past people. He got kicked and punched at as he tossed people to the floor. He didn't mean to cause any harm. He just wanted to get out. He just needed to get away. And in the end, a bouncer came along and fast-tracked his exit, dragging him out of the building and telling him to stay the hell outside at that.

He stood there in the venue, and he took a breath of that cool air. Listened to Seann's echoing footsteps. There was something else in here. It looked like some sort of safe place. Tents erected around the place. Teddy bears lying flat on their sides. Portable stoves and generators, which had long ago exhausted their worth.

"Military?" Seann asked.

Sam shrugged. "Possibly."

He walked further around this place. NRS. An arrow pointing in here. And yet... and yet it didn't seem like there was anything in here to find. Had the NRS, whoever they were, already moved on? And even if they had... Tara was on the road heading towards them, wasn't she? So surely there'd be some trace of her on that path?

He walked past one of the tents, and he saw something. A note. Handwritten. And by the side of that note, loose bullets.

He picked up the note.

It was a child's handwriting. A drawing underneath of the arena, tents, and people all standing there, and people in green who looked vaguely like military, all holding guns.

Mum says we will get out of here soon.

But the army keep saying we've got to stay cause there's bad people outside and if we get away I don't want what happened to the man with the beard to happen. It wasn't nice what happened to him.

I will see Disneyland some time soon. Mum promised me. And Mum is good and I love her and

And the note just ended, right there, just like that.

"Shit," Seann said. "Something went down here. Almost like the military had this place as some sort of safe zone. And then... and then shit just hit the fan."

Sam nodded. "There's a reason I don't trust the military."

"You don't trust fucking *anyone*, Sam."

"The military have a special place in my heart when it comes to distrust. Nothing personal. Just... well. Something I went through."

He walked over to the stage. Looked like there'd been some sort of struggle here. There was blood on the stage. It looked old. Definitely not fresh. More bullets up here, too.

"You think this is the NRS?"

Sam looked around the stage. Than at the arena beyond. "I don't know," he said. "But..."

And then he saw it.

The door. Right at the back of the stage. Backstage, quite literally.

Chains were wrapped around the handles. And scuttling at the foot of the door, Sam saw something that sent a shiver down his spine.

Insects.

He walked over to that door. Slowly. Held his breath. His heart started racing. Sometimes in life, we all get hunches when we expect we might find something. And right now, Sam had a hunch he was going to find something right behind these double doors.

He grabbed the chain. Started untying it from the door. Pulled them apart.

"Shit!" Seann shouted, his voice echoing around the arena.

Sam spun around.

He saw Seann running to the right. And he was about to ask him what the hell he was doing when he saw the movement scurrying across the stage.

"Rats," Seann said. "I fucking hate rats."

Sam smirked. Seeing Seann spooked like that was a pleasant respite from the tension.

Seann seemed to notice, too. "You find it funny?"

"Not at all," Sam said.

"Try telling your face that."

He turned back to the door, still smiling a little. But also fully aware that there was something in this room. Something unpleasant. Something he wasn't sure he wanted to find. But something he was going to be faced with very, very soon.

He held his breath. Time standing still. Not wanting to open these doors. Not wanting to see what was inside. But knowing he had to.

And then he pulled the handles.

Opened the doors.

More bugs crawled out of the room. Mice and rats scuttled away, squeaking and squealing. And he didn't notice anything else. Not at first. Not right away.

Not until that bad smell filled his lungs.

A fucking awful smell.

"Fuck," Seann said. "Jesus... What the..."

But Seann didn't finish. Or maybe he did. Sam wasn't sure.

Because staring back at him was something awful.

Something truly awful.

There were some things in life you couldn't unsee, no matter how hard you tried. Things that haunted your nightmares. That taunted you in moments of downtime.

Sam knew right away that this was one of them.

CHAPTER TWENTY

A few moments would always stick with Sam—for the wrong reasons.

The Iraq incident—obviously. That would always stay with him so much that it made him nervous just thinking about it. The day Rebecca left. Not in a boo-hoo, self-pitying way. But just in the sense that the moment broke him so much emotionally that it would always traumatise him. Always. And unfortunately, there were a bunch of other moments, too. Wayne's death. Tristan's death. Rebecca's "death" and then her return. Millie's death, most recently. To name just a few. Memories that would forever be ingrained in his consciousness and would forever haunt his psyche. That would keep him awake at night or haunt his dreams.

And he knew right now that this was one of them.

It was dark in this room. Very dark. But that didn't hide what was right in front of him. He could hear Seann behind him. It sounded like he was heaving or throwing up. And Sam couldn't blame him. The smell was ghastly.

There were people in here. They were lying on the floor. Some had cuffs around their wrists. Some had chains around their ankles. Some of them had pools of blood around their genitals. Most of them were naked, and they looked malnourished and pale.

And the scariest thing of all?

They didn't look like they'd been dead all that long.

This looked *recent*.

Sam stepped forward into the room.

"Sam," Seann said between bouts of violent heaving. "There—there ain't anything for us to see here."

But Sam wasn't listening. Because this place. This arena. It had the initials "NRS" painted on the entrance. Pointing right in this direction. So he needed to know. He needed to know for certain.

He walked from body to body. An old man. A young woman. A kid who couldn't be older than five. All of them left in here to die. Left to starve.

"Sam," Seann said. "There—there ain't anything to be gained from looking around this place."

But Sam knew that was bollocks. Sam knew Seann was just trying to protect him. Because there *was* potentially something to be gained here. There was something very fucking serious to be gained.

And that was the possibility that Tara might be in here.

He kept on moving from body to body. Kept on looking for a sign. A sign that she might be in here. A sign that she might have been in here. And he pictured what he'd do if he found her. It made him feel guilty. Because at the end of the day, this was awful as it was. This level of death at the hands of—of whoever had done this. This was fucking grim. And it was horrifying. So the fact he was actually praying Tara wasn't one of these people felt... wrong.

But wasn't that just human nature?

He kept on searching. Still no trace of her whatsoever.

"Sam," Seann said.

"Shut up."

"This place," Seann said. "It's—it's not right. Something's not right."

"Then go," Sam said.

"Fuck you," Seann said. "Fuck you."

Sam kept on searching the room. He didn't know where Seann was or what he was doing. He didn't know whether he was sticking around or whether he'd left. But he wasn't leaving this room until he'd searched every last body.

He kept on looking until he saw her.

Sitting right there, slumped over. About her height. Head down. Face out of view.

But... but it looked like her.

It fucking wounded him to admit it looked like her.

He stood there. Frozen. For a few seconds. Just staring down at her. Everything else fading into irrelevance. It was just him and her here in this awful room.

He didn't want to go over to her. He didn't want to find her dead. Because... because that wasn't how their story was supposed to end. It—it would be such a pointless end. And that's not how it was supposed to go. Especially with so much between them so unspoken. Especially with so many things to apologise for. And so many things to discuss.

His feelings towards her.

Everything.

He stood there, shaking, and he didn't want to walk up to her. He didn't want to find her dead. He wanted to walk out of this room and continue his search. Because at least that way, at least by refusing to find out whether this was her or not, he didn't know for certain. Not for definite. He could keep the search alive. He could keep his hope alive.

And really, that's what this was about, wasn't it?

If he didn't find her, there was still hope.

But as he stood there in this awful room, physically shaking, he knew he couldn't just turn his back. He knew he couldn't just walk away.

He knew it was now or never.

He closed his burning eyes.

Swallowed a lump in his throat.

And then he stepped forward, and he lifted her head.

He held it there. Felt the soft, cold skin of her face against his fingers. The heaviness of her dead head in his hands. He wanted to keep his eyes closed. He didn't want to look. Didn't want to see.

But he had to know.

He opened his eyes.

There was a woman staring back at him. The light in her eyes had gone out.

But as Sam looked into this woman's eyes, feeling desperately sorry for her, he also felt a wave of relief.

Because as tragic as this was... the woman wasn't Tara.

He stroked the poor woman's head. Stepped back. Looked around this room. Looked at this tomb where these poor people had spent their last hours and days in such pain. Such misery. He didn't know what'd gone down here or who had done this. But it wasn't good.

He just prayed to God Tara hadn't suffered like they had.

He turned around and walked out of the room and back onto the stage when suddenly he saw something right in front of him.

Seann.

He was standing in front of the stage, right there where the crowd would be.

And he wasn't alone.

CHAPTER TWENTY-ONE

Sam *knew* the arena was a death trap. He knew it was too good to be fucking true. And he knew the second he'd started walking down that corridor and deep into the belly of this place that he was taking a risk. A massive risk.

But he'd ignored his instincts. He'd pushed his gut feelings aside. And for what? For an NRS logo, sprayed on a wall outside. For a hunch that it might lead him right towards Tara. A hunch he knew fucking well he'd chastise anyone else for were the roles reversed.

And now here he was. His deepest fears—but his greatest suspicion—staring him in the face.

Seann had his hands behind his head. He wasn't holding his rifle anymore. One of the cunts who had him was holding it, pointing it at Sam.

Standing behind Seann, a man. Skinny. Bearded. Big dark circles under his eyes. Angry red sores all over his skin. A blood-shot right eye, weeping pus. He didn't look good. Didn't look in a good way at all.

But he was holding a blade to Seann's throat.

"Gonna make this nice and easy for you," Beardy said. "You're gonna drop that weapon of yours. And whatever else is in that nice rucksack over your shoulder there. And then you're gonna take a few steps back to that nice little room you just came out of while we figure out what we're gonna do with you next."

Sam shook his head. "No chance."

Beardy's eyes narrowed. He pushed the blade harder against Seann's neck, squeezing his Adam's apple. "Wasn't a request, tough guy."

"I've just spent a month of my fucking life trapped in a dark fucking room with no way out. I'll die before I go back in that room."

Beardy stared back at Sam. His eyes narrowed. Silence filled the echoey arena. "You're gonna make things difficult, huh?"

"I'm not gonna make things *anything*," Sam said. "I'm just telling you how it is. I'm not going into that room. If you want me in that room, you're gonna have to fucking drag me there. We're not... we're not here for trouble. We're here for the NRS."

"The old Northern Rebuilding Society?" Beardy said, laughing a little as he spoke. "Well, good luck with that one."

Another pause. More silence. Beardy and his minions—another five or six that Sam could see—standing there, weighing up their next move.

And then it was Beardy who spoke. "Danny, get the fuck over there and get him in that room. If he ain't gonna play ball, we're just gonna have to make him."

Danny—the man holding Seann's rifle—nodded and started walking over towards Sam. And Sam felt his heartbeat starting to pick up. Because that's what he wanted. That's *exactly* what he wanted. If he could get someone close to him... maybe he could buy himself some time.

He wasn't sure what the plan was exactly. But he knew it involved this man, Danny.

And he was walking right into his trap.

Danny lifted the rifle. Pointed it at Sam. "Drop the rifle."

Sam held his ground. "Or what?"

"Don't fuck with me," Danny said. "Rifle, on the floor, now."

Sam held tightly onto the rifle. He didn't want to drop it. He didn't want to let go.

But then he took a deep breath, lowered it to the floor. "There. Happy now?"

Danny looked back at Beardy. Almost like he was seeking advice on what to do next.

And then he looked back at Sam. "Kick it over here," he said.

Sam put his foot on the rifle. Held it there a few seconds.

"I'm not fucking about," Danny said. "Kick it over here. Now."

Sam sighed. Shook his head. "If you just asked politely..."

And then he kicked the rifle. Only he didn't kick it forward. He kicked it off to the side. Away from him and also away from Danny.

Danny's eyes narrowed. "You got a fucking death wish or something?"

"Just leave it, Danny," Beardy said.

"He's fucking with us, Gerald. Fucking with us."

"And you're letting him," Beardy—Gerald—said. "Don't let him get in your head. Just... just get him into that room. He's unarmed. What're you waiting for?"

Sam stared at Danny. Waited for him to approach. But he could see that look in Danny's eyes. He could see that uncertainty. Like Danny had caught a glimpse of Sam's true nature and knew he wasn't somebody he wanted to fuck with.

"Go on," Gerald barked. "Get the fuck on with it before I have to slit this bastard's throat."

Danny started walking. Rifle raised. Pointing right at Sam.

And Sam just stood there. Staring at Danny. Taking deep breaths, right into his belly and right out of his nostrils.

He knew he needed to try something. He knew he desperately needed to act. But he also knew that time was running out. And that if he got this wrong... well, there were no second chances. If he got this wrong, he was dead. Seann was dead. He had to get this right. He had to make it count.

He looked over Danny's shoulder as he kept on approaching. Looked at Seann. Right into his eyes. Saw him looking back at him. Wide-eyed. Knife to his throat. Hands behind his head.

"Come on," Danny said. Right in front of Sam now. "Back up."

Sam looked into Seann's eyes, and he nodded.

He took a deep breath.

Then he looked back at Danny.

"You know, you should really learn how the safety mechanism of a rifle works properly at this point, Danny."

Danny's eyes widened. "What—"

Sam grabbed the rifle and slammed it back into Danny's face.

Danny's nose cracked. He tried to pull the trigger, but nothing happened. He fell back, hit the floor of the stage.

Sam yanked the rifle from his hands. Removed the safety. And then he pressed the rifle to Danny's head as he lay there on the stage. He looked up at Gerald, who still had the knife pressed to Seann's neck. Wide-eyed. Shocked. The rest of his people staring up this way in shock, too.

"Now," Sam said, holding his rifle to Danny's head. "How about we have a grown-up fucking conversation here?"

CHAPTER TWENTY-TWO

Sam held the rifle to the head of the bastard on the floor in front of him and felt the tables turning in his favour.

The man beneath him—Danny—kept wriggling around, trying to break free.

"Stay still," Sam said. Pushing the rifle down further, so hard he felt he might crack his skull like an easter egg. "Don't move a fucking muscle, or I'll blow your brains out."

"Fuck you," Danny shouted. But he stopped wriggling about, which told Sam he was scared enough to start complying. Good. That's exactly where he wanted this bastard.

Gerald held the blade to Seann's throat. He looked a bit more alarmed now. A bit more worried and panicked. He hadn't seen that coming, the fucking prick. Not so tough anymore.

"Here's how this is going to go," Sam shouted as he stood there on the stage of the arena, staring down at his audience. Gerald, Seann, and a few other people in the background, who were frozen to the spot. "You let Seann go. Right this fucking second. And we walk out of here. That's how it's going to go."

Gerald shook his head. "It's not happening, buddy."

Sam pushed the rifle down hard against Danny's head. "If it doesn't, this man dies. Your friend here dies."

"Please," Danny begged; tough guy act well and truly discarded now. "I—I didn't want this shit. I never—I never wanted this shit."

Gerald narrowed his eyes. Kept that blade to Seann's neck. Stared up at Sam. Sam could see a little blood trickling down Seann's neck. He knew if he wasn't careful, if he didn't play this right, that bastard was going to kill Seann right in front of him.

"Gerald," Danny shouted. "Stop—stop this, man. Just—just fucking stop this."

"You'd be wise listening to your friend here," Sam said. "Or does his life mean fuck all to you, too?"

Something shifted in Gerald when he said those words. He glanced over his shoulder at the others he was here with. One of them started walking back, heading towards the arena doors.

"Stop," Sam shouted.

Gerald shook his head. "Don't listen to him—"

"You move another muscle and you're dead, and so is everyone. Understand? Stop. Right this fucking second."

"Don't..." Gerald started.

But it was already too late. Because his friend had stopped.

"Alvin?" Gerald said.

Alvin shook his head. "This shit's gone on far too long, Gerald," he said. "It's over. We've—we've bitten off more than we can chew. Just let the fuckers walk. What use are two dudes anyway?"

Gerald blushed.

Sam narrowed his eyes. Pushed the rifle against Danny's head even harder. "What's it going to be?"

Gerald didn't say a word. He just stood there. Staring up at Sam like he was thinking this through. Figuring out just how much he was willing to lose here.

And then, finally, he spoke.

"Kill him," Gerald said.

"What?" Sam said.

"What?" Danny shouted. "I—no! Don't! You cunt! You—you cunt!"

"Kill him," Gerald said. "He's nothing to us anyway. But let me get something straight here." He dragged Seann's head back, exposing his neck, which was already a little cut. "You kill him, I kill your friend here. An eye for an eye. That's just the way of the world, isn't it?"

Fuck. Sam wasn't expecting this fucker to call his bluff. He was hoping Gerald valued this guy's life enough to start playing ball. Maybe he *was* bluffing. But it was hard to tell. It was a different fucking game now. And not one Sam wanted to play.

"Go on," Gerald shouted. "Kill him. Kill him if that's what you want. But you know what it means. Not just for him. Or me. But for your friend here. And for you. 'Cause we've got other people, matey. We've got other people out there. And if you think you're just gonna walk away from this... you're mistaken. Very mistaken."

Sam felt trapped. Cornered. Because if this guy really did have people outside, he was in danger. And although he wasn't usually one to crumble in the face of danger, he thought about Tara. If Tara was still out there—which she was—and if she was with Kurt... then he needed to stay alive. He needed to stay alive because he was the last fucking person left who had an opportunity to find her and potentially save her.

He looked down at Danny, lying there on the floor. Crying. Whimpering. And although he hated this prick for crossing him, he saw the humanity in his desperate, bloodshot eyes. The way he squinted up at Sam, begging him. "Please. Please."

Sam looked up at Gerald. At Seann. At the way Gerald was holding that knife to Seann's neck.

"Come on," Gerald said. "Put the poor man out of his misery. If we're all going out together, then you be the man to make that first shot. You be the man to pull that trigger. If that's how you really want to handle this."

Sam looked down at Danny again. He squeezed the trigger, gently. And then he heard struggling up ahead and saw Gerald was pressing that blade down harder against Seann's neck now. Getting so close to slicing his throat.

"Go on," Gerald said. "Why don't we have a little countdown, hmm? Both kill on three?"

"Please," Danny begged, whimpering. "Please."

Sam looked down at him.

He tightened his grip around the trigger.

And then he thought about Tara and thought about the best road out of this mess.

"No?" Gerald said. "You not gonna be the first. Ahh, well. Let me get things started."

And just like that, in the space of a second, Gerald pulled back the blade and swung it at Seann's throat.

CHAPTER TWENTY-THREE

Sam watched the blade hurtle towards Seann's throat.

And as he stood there on the stage of this arena like he was having an out-of-body experience, watching Gerald prepare to kill Seann, he felt this void inside him. The sense of failure. This sense of letting somebody else down. Of failing to save yet another of his people.

And then something altogether different happened.

Something completely unexpected.

Gerald lowered the knife.

He pushed Seann down. Pushed him down, so he was face flat on the arena floor.

"*Here's* how shit's gonna go," Gerald said. "You and your friend are gonna get the fuck out of here right now. You're gonna leave those rifles behind. You're gonna leave those rucksacks behind. But you're gonna go. You're gonna walk away. Right now."

Sam couldn't actually believe what he was hearing. He'd braced himself to watch Seann die right in front of him—not the first person to die right in front of him. And now here Gerald was, telling him he was letting him go? That he was letting Seann go, too?

"You walk away, the pair of you. You leave. Right now. And you never come back here. Never. Unless... well. Unless you've got something for us. In which case, you're more than welcome."

"Gerald?" one of the blokes muttered. "Are—are you sure?"

"I'm sure," Gerald said. "They have supplies. That'll do for now. As long as they leave. And as long as they leave immediately."

Sam still couldn't believe this, as he stood there, holding the gun to Danny's head. He was just going to let him and Seann go like this? It seemed mental. This just wasn't how this shit went. Not usually.

Only... something felt wrong. Something felt so off about it. Something was ringing serious alarm bells in Sam's mind and making him feel mistrustful. So fucking mistrustful.

"Get the fuck out of here. Walk away. Right this fucking second. But you do not lay a finger on my friend there. You do not hurt my people."

"Thank you," Danny muttered. "Thank—thank you."

"We'll deal with you internally, Danny," Gerald said. "For how you spoke about me. But for now..." He looked back at Sam. "What are you waiting for?"

Sam looked down at Gerald. He looked at the people standing around him. And he looked at Seann, lying flat on the arena floor.

"I'm not dicking around here," Gerald said. "This is what you wanted. Isn't it?"

Sam looked down at Gerald now as he held the rifle in his hand. He looked at Seann. He looked at everyone here, and he saw a possibility opening up in front of him. A means of escape developing right before his eyes. Because Gerald had shown his hand. He'd shown how loyal to his people he was. And he'd shown his weakness. But Sam didn't for a second expect Gerald to let him go like he was promising. He was just doing it to stop him from shooting Danny here. And he wasn't falling for it.

But that's where he'd fucked up.

"Go," Gerald said. "Walk away. But leave your stuff. Now!"

Sam swallowed a lump in his throat.

He took a deep breath.

"One thing you should know about me," he said.

Gerald frowned. "And what's that?"

"I don't take nicely to being given orders."

And then he lifted the rifle, and he shot Gerald in the head.

The gunshot echoed around the arena. He heard Danny crying beneath him, and he pointed the rifle at him and shot him, too, right through the head.

Then he lifted and pointed at the rest of Gerald's people, all running around like headless fucking chickens, and he fired at them.

One, by one, by one.

Fired at them as they tried to seek cover, as they tried to escape.

And he didn't hold back one bit.

He saw Seann jumping to his feet when suddenly Gerald sparked back to life. The bullet. It hadn't hit his head after all. Must've hit his throat. He was bleeding from it. Bleeding badly. Blood spurting out of it, seeping between his fingers.

But he was standing. And he was lifting his knife in his shaking hand, and he was swinging it at Seann.

Sam took a breath.

He focused on Gerald.

So close to Seann. So, so close to Seann. So close that if he wasn't careful, the bullet might just fucking hit Seann instead.

But he took another one of those deep breaths.

He told himself this was what he had to do. That he had absolutely no other choice.

And then, with total focus, he fired.

The bullet splattered through the side of Gerald's head.

Gerald's eyes twitched up into his skull. Blood exploded out of his temple. He twitched and shook for a moment, and then he fell to the floor below.

Sam looked around the arena, the echoes of gunshots ringing in his ears. He grabbed the rifle from the stage and hopped off, running over to Seann. He held out a hand to him as he crouched there on his knees, wide-eyed. Staring at the bloodbath. Outside somewhere, Sam could hear shouting echoing closer towards the arena. More of their people. Fuck.

"Come on," Sam said, holding out a hand to Seann. "Time we got out of here."

Seann looked up at him. But he looked distant. He looked miles away.

"Come on," Sam said. "We don't have much more time. We've got to go."

And as Seann sat there on his knees, looking around at the bloodbath of Sam's making, blood splattered down his own face... he looked afraid. He looked genuinely afraid.

"Now," Sam said. "We need to get out of here."

Seann looked at Sam's hand.

And then, without taking it, he stood.

It was time to get out of this arena.

It was time to get out of this bloodbath.

But as Sam ran, Seann by his side, it was Danny's final whimpers he couldn't get out of his mind—and that fearful look in his eyes as he'd pulled the trigger.

A few moments would always stick with Sam—for the wrong reasons.

This was just another.

CHAPTER TWENTY-FOUR

Seann didn't say a word to Sam after they left the arena.

It was getting late. Felt like it'd been a long day. A long and eventful day. The discovery of Tara's note. The NRS, who he knew was a group now—the Northern Rebuilding Society, something far less catchy and mysterious than he was imagining. And the shit that went down with Gerald and his group. Yeah. It'd been eventful. But they were still here. They were still alive. They'd left the arena without attracting any attention from anyone else. They had to count themselves lucky.

Seann was really quiet. He hadn't even looked Sam in the eye since they'd walked away from the arena. Going out of his way to avoid talking to him, which Sam found odd. He'd pretty much saved the ungrateful bastard's life. What was his problem?

But then he didn't want to *ask* what his problem was. He didn't want to get involved in any sort of argument or debate right now. He just wanted to find somewhere to shelter for a few hours, then start up their search again. The search for the NRS. The search for Kurt. The search for Tara.

He saw an old bus station in the distance. Looked pretty derelict. Not the biggest he'd ever seen. Might provide a bit of shelter for a few hours, which would be helpful considering it was raining a bit now.

"How's that place look?" Sam asked.

Seann shrugged.

Sam gritted his teeth and tried to resist Seann's silent treatment bait, but he couldn't help himself. "What the fuck's your problem?"

Seann glared at him. "What the fuck is *my* problem?"

"You're walking around like someone's pissed in your Corn Flakes. What's that all about?"

"You almost killed me, Sam. You almost got me killed."

"What?" Sam said. "Bollocks. I saved your frigging life."

"No," Seann said. "You pulled that trigger, and you risked shooting me."

"If I hadn't bloody shot Gerald, you'd be dead now."

"Before then. Gerald said he was letting us go."

"Gerald would've had us locked away in that hell room the second I dropped my rifle."

"We don't know that."

"How fucking dumb are you?" Sam shouted.

Seann just stood there shaking his head. "You didn't have to slaughter the lot of them like that."

Sam puffed out his lips. "I can't actually believe you're saying this. I cannot believe what I'm hearing."

"But it's true, isn't it?"

Sam rolled his eyes. "If I hadn't killed them, they would've come after us. I still can't fucking believe we're even having this debate—"

"We shouldn't have even been in that place."

"Oh, fuck off."

"But we went in there because you just had to risk everything to find her, didn't you?"

"Don't bring her into it."

"I'm not having you shutting me down anymore. I'm here

because I'm helping you. But if I'm helping you... this can't just be a one-way fucking street. Not anymore."

"Stop being dramatic."

"You're so fucking terrified, aren't you?"

Sam frowned. "What?"

"I can see it. You're so fucking terrified of losing the people you care about that you're going to get other people killed in the process. Me included. And if you don't wake the fuck up fast, you're going to get somebody *else* killed. Wake up, Sam. Wake the fuck up."

He walked past Sam, then. And Sam shook his head. "Cunt," he muttered.

But as Seann walked past, Sam couldn't shake the thought nagging at his mind like a mosquito buzzing around him in the sun.

The thought that Seann might be right.

CHAPTER TWENTY-FIVE

am sat in the darkness and listened to the flames crackling in front of him.

It was late. He and Seann had found a detached house just outside town to shelter for the night—or a few hours of the night, anyway. It felt pretty cold outside as they sat around this fire. A sure sign that autumn was approaching and that summer was coming to its end. Fuck, the thought of another winter was not a good one. He wasn't sure he was going to survive it. And he figured everyone who was fortunate—or unfortunate—enough to still be here would all have the same concerns looming large.

He looked at the flames flickering before him. They were in the back yard of this house. He never liked setting fires. They attracted unnecessary attention. Attention he'd rather not draw towards himself. He knew what it was like whenever he saw a fire burning in the middle of nowhere. A part of him felt intimidated by it. But another part of him was *drawn* to it like a moth to a flame. Only we all know what happens to the moth in that scenario, don't we?

He listened to those crackling flames. It relaxed him. Comforted him. But there was something about it that made him feel more vulnerable, too. There was something primitive about sitting around a fire like this, wasn't there? It awoke something inside him he usually kept so covered up. So suffocated.

He looked up at Seann. Seann hadn't said much since they'd got here. And Sam felt kind of bad for how he'd spoken to him earlier. And he felt bad in general for how he'd treated him. Seann had given up a hell of a lot to be here with him. He'd risked his life to help him find Tara. He'd stuck around, even through all their difficulties. And Sam had treated him like total shit.

"You alright?" Sam asked. Avoiding eye contact as well as he could.

Seann glanced up at him. Nodded.

"What happened," Sam said. "Back at the arena. I... I was rash. You're right. I should've... I should've been less hasty. I should've shown more caution. I should've shown more care. But I... I put us at risk. Both of us. And even though I got us out of it..."

"Just had to slip that last bit in there, didn't you?"

"*We* got out of it," Sam said. "But I... I should never have got us into that mess in the first place. I'm... I'm sorry."

Seann looked at him. Stared right into his eyes. Really studied him.

And then he took a deep breath. Sighed. "Right at the start of this blackout, it was just me and my partner, Colin. I... I loved him. A lot. And I'm not a lovey-dovey person. Takes a lot for me to open up. To let people in. Childhood shit. Dad never accepting me for who I was. Mum wasn't much better. You know the story already. You've heard it a million times before."

Sam nodded. Listening to Seann.

"But Colin... I... I loved him. Really loved him. We had a good relationship. We were different. He was *quiet* for one."

"Really different, then."

"Shut up. But yeah. He was quiet. He was... stoic, somehow.

And I don't know. I guess he made me feel comfortable. And I guess he made me feel like it was truly okay. To be me."

He stopped. Paused a second. Quite clearly swallowing a lump in his throat.

"One day, I woke up, and he—he was just gone. No trace of him. Just—just got up and left. And... and I searched for him. This was early days, still. Plenty of people still about. I searched. I searched and searched. I clutched at every single trace of him I could find. I put... I put myself in so much danger to try and find him. Even though... even though deep in my mind, I knew I was never going to find him again. I just... I just couldn't come to terms with the possibility of a life without him. And that... that almost destroyed me. Almost."

Sam felt the weight of guilt building up inside him even more. Fuck. He'd been a prick with Seann. Especially with everything he'd been through.

"I... There was someone else, too. Someone else I was close to. Someone called Tate. I... I got close to him some time after the collapse. I let my guard drop, just as I swore I never would. And they... This group of thugs. They murdered him. They murdered him right in front of me. I was driven by revenge. But I —I realised that no matter how hard I tried, no matter how hard I sought out revenge... I was never going to get it. And it was never going to bring Tate back."

He paused for a second. Stared out to space.

"I'll never find Colin again," Seann said. "And I'll never bring Tate back. That's... that's something I've come to accept. But it wasn't an easy road there. And if I could take that road again and do things differently... I would. I would do so much differently."

He looked at Sam, right across those flames.

"I'm not asking you to stop searching for Tara. Because paradoxical as it sounds, a part of me regrets giving up on Tate, too. Even though my journey had to stop, I wish I'd been less rash. I wish I'd searched more methodically. I wish I hadn't been blinded by this quest to find him at all costs and just stopped to take a breath sometime. Because if I had… I dunno. Maybe I'd have found something."

Sam listened to Seann's words. He took them in. And he felt them. He really felt them deep inside. Speaking to him.

"Life's completely out of control," Seann said. "You can only do your best. That's all you can ever do."

He looked back at the flames. Sam stared at those flames, too. And as he sat there, in the darkness of night, he heard Seann, loud and clear.

He was not going to give up on his search for Tara.

But he needed to remember not to lose himself—or Seann—in the process.

CHAPTER TWENTY-SIX

Carlton looked around at the bodies of his companions—of his friends—and he felt a wave of anger build up inside.

It was late. Although here in the darkness of the arena, it could be any time of day at all. He could hear a little rain falling against the roof. Weird being in an arena like this and hearing how silent it was. The last time he'd been in an arena, he'd taken his niece to a Bruno Mars gig. He kind of wanted to linger at the back, but she insisted they made their way right to the front. Stuck out like a sore thumb, he did. Thirty-five-year-old man, completely unenthusiastic, surrounded by wild teenage girls. Yeah. Not exactly the most comfortable environment, and certainly not ideal for a self-conscious douchebag like him.

But he didn't take his niece to these gigs out of the kindness of his heart. He took her because he wanted to sleep with her.

He wasn't sure how it began. This weird fascination he had with her. She just seemed... different from other women. He had a wife, sure. Sally. She was alright, really. Pretty. Kind. But there was just something so... *safe* about her. And his niece, his Cady, seemed so cool, so alluring, so *dangerous*. And that's what drew him to her.

And she was eighteen now. She was eighteen, so technically, it was okay. Technically, legally, it was fine. Right? It was fine.

But Carlton knew deep down he had a sickness. A deep, deep sickness right at his core.

He didn't have to worry about Cady anymore. He didn't have to worry about the pass he'd made at her and how she'd gone straight to her mum and told her. He didn't have to worry about any of the potential family repercussions or the threats of police involvement. In some ways, the blackout had come at exactly the right time for him.

And standing here now, all that felt like an eternity ago.

Especially staring at these bodies. Lying here in front of him. Dead.

He saw Danny lying there on the stage. He had been shot in the head. Fragments of skull stuck out like broken meringue. One of his eyes dangled out of the cracked remains of his broken head.

And it wasn't just Danny. Stu. Francis. But also... also, Gerald.

Their leader, as much as it pained Carlton to ever admit it. Because—because things hadn't been great lately in their group. Things hadn't been ideal. They were growing short of supplies. The usual smuggling routes were running thin. A few of the groups they relied on for trade had gone quiet. And suddenly, out of nowhere, Carlton and his group were starving and struggling and being forced to change their strategy completely. Forced to leave their home. And he knew Gerald was just caving to popular opinion. He knew that even though Gerald liked to pretend he was strong, deep down, he wasn't all that strong. He was weak. He was a leader by accident. And he was getting weaker all the time.

But now, here they were. Staring at the bodies of the fallen. It'd all happened so fast. It'd all fallen apart so quickly.

That man. That man with the gun.

Pulling the trigger.

Firing them all down.

And then running away.

Running away while just the four of them lived. Him, Mary, Simon, and Harry.

"What do we do?"

A voice. A voice right by his side. Mary. Looking at *him*. And then Carlton realised she wasn't the only one looking at him. Simon, too. And Harry. Looking at him like he was their leader now. Looking at him like he was the one they were turning to.

Carlton looked up at the stage. Then he looked around at the empty void of the arena, at the many seats surrounding them, and then out of the door in the direction those fuckers had disappeared.

And right there before him, he saw an opportunity. He saw a chance. A chance for a reset. A chance to start again.

And there was only one place to start.

"We're going to find those men," he said. "And we're going to make them pay. For what they've done to our people."

CHAPTER TWENTY-SEVEN

Tara saw Kurt lying by her side and she knew tonight was the best opportunity she was ever going to get to kill him.

It was pitch black. She could hear the wind howling outside and the rain falling heavily on the roof of the house. And Kurt was lying there, right in front of her. Right on that bed. She'd been here before. She'd found herself in this kind of situation before. Standing over Kurt, faced with the chance of running away—or of killing him.

But this... this felt different.

Because it *was* different.

It was different because she was holding a blade in her hand.

She stood over him. Shaking. Her hand felt all clammy, and her grip felt weak. Her heart wouldn't stop racing. As she stood over Kurt, she didn't know what was stopping her. This man was a monster. This man had caused immeasurable pain to her. And to people she cared about. And now she had a chance. Now, she had an opportunity. Now, she had an opportunity to finish him off and get away from him, once and for all.

So why was she still standing here, standing over him?

And what was holding her back?

She swallowed a thick, phlegmy lump in her throat. It was simple. She just needed to lift that knife. She needed to lift that knife, and she needed to bury it in this bastard's throat. It would be so simple. So quick. So clean. Well, not *clean* exactly, but you get the picture.

And yet... despite all her anger, despite her rage, despite her lust for revenge, and despite knowing this monster did not value her life one bit... she was still just standing over him. Holding that knife.

And you know what it was?

It was that fear.

That fear that there was something more to this.

That fear that this wasn't the end.

That fear that she was making a big, big mistake. And yet she couldn't even explain why.

She was exhausted. She was weak. She was shaking. She had no idea where she was, only they were heading north to some NRS place, whatever the fuck that was, and whoever the fuck they were. Was she going to keep heading to that place when she was on her own? Was she going to keep going like that? She wasn't sure. She didn't know at all.

She just knew that when she got away from Kurt... at least then, she'd be free again. Because she wasn't some subservient woman. She wasn't the property of men. She'd been put through hell by men for far too many years. She'd been treated like shit far too many times. And she hated the thought that she was someone who needed "saving" or whatever the fuck like that. Absolutely fucking despised it.

She was going to get away from Kurt. She was going to get away from this monster. And whatever she did next, she was going to be independent. Not in a cliché "girl power" way. But she was going to live the life she'd always wanted to live, even if the reality of this world made that very, very difficult.

She pulled back the knife, held her breath, and went to swing it towards Kurt's neck when suddenly he opened his eyes.

His hand shot out with a surprising force. He grabbed her wrist and squeezed it tight before pulling her down towards him. She clutched on to that knife, her grip on it loosening every second.

He stared at her as he held her with that surprising strength for someone so skinny. A smile stretched across his face. And it felt like he'd planned this. It felt like a nightmare. It felt like he knew she was awake, and she was standing over him, and that she was going to try killing him. It was like this was exactly what she'd been fearing all along.

He punched her, then. Punched her across the room, again with surprising force. Sent her flying back across the floor, the knife still in her grip, still *just* in her grip. If she could just stand up, if she could just get to her feet, if she could just swing it at him in time, then maybe she could put this fucker down. Maybe this wasn't over. Maybe—

And then he leapt on top of her.

Before she could pull back her wrist—before she could do *anything* at all—he was on top of her. Holding both her arms. Knees buried into her stomach, pushing the air out of her body. And there he was. Looking down at her. Smiling. And she wondered if this was it. She wondered if this was finally the moment he raped her. It hadn't happened yet, but it always happened eventually, didn't it? Men like Kurt were sick. They always found a way to justify their cruellest actions to themselves, and they always had.

She watched him watch *her* as she tried to struggle free. As she tried to break her hands and her wrists and her body free. She watched his smile grow as her efforts dwindled. She saw the smug satisfaction on his face as she tried to squeeze free of him, as she tried to kick and tried to punch and even tried to bite.

And she saw his smile widen even more as she gave up.

"That's it," he said. "That's right."

"Fuck you," Tara gasped. But it was a weak, pained gasp.

Kurt laughed a little. "When will you get the message? When will it finally click? You aren't getting away, Tara. You're not in control. You're nowhere near in control. It ends when I *say* it ends. Not when you've had enough. When *I've* had enough. And believe me. I've nowhere near done with you yet."

She stared up at him. Heart racing. Thought about lunging forward and wrapping her teeth around his throat.

She expected him to punch her. She expected him to tear her clothes off. She expected all kinds of horrible possibilities.

But in the end, something rather different happened.

He stood up. Brushed himself down. And he held out a hand.

"Come on," he said. "Back to your feet."

Tara stared at him. Heart thumping. She wasn't sure what to say or what to think. "I–"

"I'm sorry," Kurt said. "For hitting you. But you... you left me with no choice. I'm working on... I'm working on it. Okay?"

She looked up into his black void eyes, and she swore she heard something in his voice that made her feel even more uneasy.

Sincerity.

She didn't want to take his hand. She didn't want his help.

But right now, she found herself putting her hand in his.

And then, gently, he lifted her back to her feet. Looked into her eyes. Smiled.

"Come on," he said. "Get some sleep. It'll... It'll all just be a memory in the morning."

And then he walked back to the bed like nothing had happened at all.

Tara stood there. Shaking. Lump swelling in her throat.

Because as much as she wanted to get away from this monster, she couldn't shake a feeling niggling at the back of her mind.

A feeling that this man was better at what he did than Jonno. Better at *control* than Jonno.

And she was never going to get away from him.

CHAPTER TWENTY-EIGHT

Sam woke to the smell of burned meat.

The second he opened his eyes and saw the darkness surrounding him, he thought for one horrifying moment that he was back in the warehouse. Trapped. Blindfolded. Locked away. That smell of meat, the sound of screaming, that nightmare he'd lived for one long, horrifying month. A nightmare he never wanted to revisit. A nightmare he never wanted to experience again. Maybe he was still locked there. Maybe everything since—the journey with Seann, the search for the NRS, the search for Tara—maybe *that* was all a dream.

Only... no. He wasn't in that warehouse. He was somewhere else now.

He was in a house somewhere. Lying on a sofa. Cold leather. Not comfortable at all. And his back ached like mad. One of the perils of getting older—not that he was ancient or anything, but still something that he noticed as the days went on. Of course, living in an EMP-struck world could hardly be helping. He didn't have the luxuries of his old life. And he missed them, sometimes.

But he wasn't in that hellhole. That was something worth celebrating right now.

He looked up. Realised, actually, it wasn't as dark as he'd first thought. The curtains of this dusty lounge he was in were pulled shut, but he could see the sun shining behind them.

And standing over him, he could see Seann.

Seann was holding a plate of something. Two plates, actually. The plates didn't look so clean, which was a little off-putting. And a few flies were buzzing around.

But on that plate in front of Sam, he saw something that really captured his attention.

"Made breakfast," Seann said.

Sam picked up the plate. Saw the meat in front of him, which wasn't actually all that burned at all. It looked... decent, in all truth. Nicely cooked. "What is it?"

"It'd be better if you don't know," Seann said.

Sam glared at him. "After being trapped by cannibals for a month? Come on. Tell me. Shit like that has a way of turning a man into a fussy eater."

Seann rolled his eyes. "It's—it's hedgehog, okay?"

"Hedgehog? You absolute fucking savage."

"It was already dead. For the record. I would never kill a hedgehog."

"Roadkill for breakfast. Nice."

"It's fresh," Seann said. "Looks like it's been hit by a car or something. Which is a joke. Obviously. Because there's not really any cars about anymore."

"Hilarious," Sam said. "An awkward extension of my roadkill joke. But I'll hand it to you. It smells... interesting."

"I'm a decent cook."

"So you've told me before."

"If you don't want it, I'll happily eat it."

Sam shook his head. "It's fine. It looks... alright, actually."

"'Alright, actually.' Sounds like you're finally warming to me."

"Don't push your luck."

He ate the hedgehog meat, which fucked with his morals far

more than he expected it to. It was quite nice. Tender in the middle, crispy on the outside. And...

"Is that *spice?*" Sam asked.

Seann smiled. "Special ingredient."

"We're at the end of the world, and you're *seasoning* your food?"

"Why wouldn't I? The power might be out. But why deprive ourselves of life's greatest pleasures?"

"You're not trying to seduce me, are you?"

Seann's face dropped. "No, you raging homophobe. Just because I'm gay doesn't mean I'm automatically trying to sleep with you. Welcome to the twenty-first century, Granddad."

"I'm just kidding," Sam said. "But I figure locker room banter ain't exactly all that funny after all."

Seann shrugged as he ate his food. "To be honest, I never had a problem with it. People take the piss out of each other all the time. Couldn't give a shit what anyone said about me as long as it's not actively, like, malicious."

"The world could learn a hell of a lot from someone like you."

"Wow," Seann said, smiling. "Another compliment. Really on form today, aren't you?"

Sam shook his head, smiling a little. And as he sat there in Seann's company, he began to realise he had been harsh on this guy. He'd been way too harsh. "I do appreciate it," Sam said.

Seann shrugged. "I like cooking anyway."

"Not the food. Being here. Choosing to... to come with me. To help find Tara. I've never... I've never really properly had the chance to thank you."

"You've had tons of chances, Sam."

"I'm making a sincere point here. Take it."

Seann shrugged again. "It's okay. I figured you're not the emotional heart on the sleeve type a while ago."

"You could've walked away. You could've left me to it. Why didn't you?"

Seann took a moment. Like he was really thinking Sam's question through.

"I suppose... I suppose part of me felt like I owed Tara. Because I was the one who told her to follow me in the woods that day. I was the one who took Millie and Marky away and tried to protect them. I was... I was the one who failed them. All of them. And there's a bit of a sense of responsibility there because of that.

"But also... I don't know. I mean, what's life without a sense of purpose? What's the point if we don't have, like, a *goal* at all? There's just nothing, is there? And I figure... I figure that's not really a life for me."

Sam looked at Seann as he ate his food. And as they sat there in this dark, dusty room, the sun peeking through the curtains, he found himself nodding.

"Whatever we find," Sam said. "Or whatever... whatever we don't find. We've got this. Right? We've got it."

Seann smiled. He nodded back at him. "Starting to think you're the one who's trying to seduce *me* now with all this soppy shit."

Sam laughed. Seann laughed. The pair sat there together, eating this fucking hedgehog, and they laughed.

Sam might've lost everything. But right now, for a split second, he felt like he'd gained a friendship.

CHAPTER TWENTY-NINE

Carlton wasn't sure how long he and the others had been searching when he finally felt like it might be time to give up.

It was morning. They'd been on the road all night. Searching for any trace of the bastards who'd murdered their people. The bastards. The murderous fucking bastards. He wasn't going to let those fuckers get away with it. And he wouldn't sleep until he got the revenge he craved.

But the problem was he needed sleep. So too did his people. The three of them left, anyway. They were coming along with him and on board at the beginning because they wanted revenge, and they wanted to make those two bastards pay for what they'd done.

But as the night drew on, and it became progressively clear that they weren't going to find them, hope began to expire.

His feet were sore. Covered in blisters. Every single step was a goddamned pain. Mum used to tell him he was weaker than the other kids. That he needed to be careful and shouldn't go wandering too far because he had his health issues. And it used to bug Carlton no end. 'Cause he didn't think he had any health issues. Sure didn't know what they were, anyway.

But Mum mentioning them was enough to make him worry. Enough to send him into a panic. And enough to make the other kids tease him about it, too.

So that made him all the more determined not to seem weak. Not to seem like a pussy. And that seemed to stick with him right through until his adult life. He didn't want to give up. He didn't want to accept what was seeming more abundantly clear every single second. That he wasn't going to find the two men. And that he wouldn't be able to find them and punish them for what they'd done. And that he was going to fail his first job as leader of these people, and that they weren't gonna let him get away with that or forget it.

He looked around. Saw how his people looked at him. Saw the look on Simon's face. On Mary's face. On Harry's face. All looking sceptical. All questioning whether they'd picked the wrong guy to lead—and when to seize the initiative and start leading for themselves.

And the worst part about all this? Deep down, Carlton couldn't shake the feeling that maybe they were right. Maybe there was someone better qualified to lead than him. Maybe they could do way, way better than him.

But here he was. He was still their leader. For now, he was still their leader.

He went to turn around. Part of him wanting to admit defeat. Part of him wanting to give the fuck up.

But when he looked ahead, he noticed something.

Something that stopped him in his tracks.

Up in the distance, out of nowhere, as the morning light continued to build, he saw a house.

And in front of that house, he saw something that made him forget about all his pains and concerns—and every fucking thing.

Right in front of that house, he saw two men. Walking away from the house. Walking down the street. Two men he recognised well. Very well.

He stood there. Waited. Watched as they walked away. And then he took a deep breath, and he smiled.

"We sorting 'em out?" Mary said.

Carlton looked right at them and swallowed a lump in his throat. "Soon," he said. "Very, very soon."

They were going to follow them.

They were going to wait for the perfect opportunity.

And they were going to make them regret ever crossing their people.

CHAPTER THIRTY

Sam wasn't sure how much longer he and Seann had been walking since leaving the house, but he was beginning to lose hope.

It was early afternoon. All that mattered was finding a trace of the NRS. *Any* trace of this group and where they were. Because finding a trace of the NRS meant finding a trace of Tara. Of finding a trace of Kurt. And right now, it felt like that time was running out.

The weather was taking a turn for the worse, too. The clouds were really thick overhead. It was getting a bit windy. Didn't seem too bad at first. But started to pick up, started to get even worse as the day was progressing. Started to feel like it would develop into a full-blown storm. And that was the last thing Sam wanted right now. Literally the last fucking thing. Because that was going to hinder their journey. Never underestimate just how much of a journey-kill a storm can actually be.

He looked down the road. Looked at the buildings either side of the street. The old pub boarded up. He looked at the car mechanics, shutters pulled down over it. He looked for any sign of movement. Any sign of life. But he still couldn't see anything. Or anyone. And while he'd spent so long trying to avoid other people... today was different. Today, he *wanted* to find people. He was getting desperate. He knew he needed to be patient because you couldn't rush these things. But it felt like the more time passed, the more the chance of finding Tara was running out.

And he knew it was absurd. Because, like, she'd been in Kurt's company for God knows how long. At least, he *assumed* she had, anyway. She might've broken out of his clutches. She might've fought free. He didn't know. Didn't have a fucking clue. For all he knew, he could be heading in the wrong direction completely.

But what was he supposed to do? Ignore all the signs in front of him? The signs that Tara was heading north, towards the NRS, and that Kurt was with her?

Or what if... what if it was already too late?

That was a thought he hadn't been considering. It was a thought he'd tried to avoid considering for quite some time. The possibility that something might've happened to Tara... that was something he was trying to turn away from. Something he was trying to bury. But it was something creeping to the surface now, slowly but surely. It was a possibility he didn't want to consider. A possibility he wanted to run from. That he wanted to hide from.

But he couldn't bury his head in the sand forever.

He saw Seann turn around. Saw him look at him. That look on his face. That familiar expression. An expression he'd seen a ton of times before. And somehow, it didn't irritate Sam as much this time. Because he knew Seann wasn't just being a prick. He'd seen the real Seann more recently. Not the Seann he thought he knew. The real Seann, with his own concerns and his own traumas. And he'd seen the real Seann, who had stood by him. Who had joined him on this journey. Who had supported him. Properly, fully supported him through all sorts of shit.

He was still here. He could've walked away a ton of times, but he was still here. And it was about damned time he started properly appreciating that.

"This weather," Seann said. Battered by the wind. "It's not getting any better."

"I can see that much."

Seann sighed. "Don't—don't you think it'd make sense if we—"

"No," Sam said.

"Aren't you going to let me finish?"

"I know what you're going to say already. You're going to say we need to stop. Or we need to slow down. Or we need to do anything *but* keep on walking. Because that's what you're like. Sometimes I wonder if you even want to make any fucking progress at all."

Seann just rolled his eyes. Didn't say anything. He was clearly learning that arguing with Sam was a pretty futile exercise at this stage.

But then he started speaking again. "For all we know, Kurt might've run into the same problem."

"What?" Sam asked. To be honest, he was just about done with talking. The wind was so strong that it was taking his breath away, and the last thing he wanted to do right now was witter on.

"I'm just saying," Seann said. "We're walking like we know exactly what Kurt and Tara's movements are. We're walking like we know anything at all. All we know is that, at some point, they were together. And at some point, they were heading this way. And that's it. That's... that's literally it."

"You've changed your tune. Again."

"I've not changed my tune at all—"

"Come on," Sam said. "It's windy, like you said. It's looking stormy. The sooner we can crack on and find the NRS, the better. There's plenty of daylight left today."

Seann opened his mouth. He looked like he was going to argue. Looked like he was going to bite back.

And before he could... it was Sam who spoke. "Look," he said. "Obviously if shit gets too intense, we'll... we'll find shelter. I'm not being reckless here. I hear you. Really, I do. But for now... we keep going. Okay?"

Seann's eyes lit up a little. It was actually quite fucking heart-warming. Like he appreciated what Sam was saying. Like he appreciated he was even consulting for his opinion.

"You're probably right," Seann said. "Besides. This place always was a ropey neighbourhood. We could do far more upmarket than—"

He stopped speaking.

In an instant, he stopped speaking.

Because from one of the buildings on their right, he heard something—and Sam heard something—that made him freeze on the spot.

Out of nowhere, Sam heard a scream.

CHAPTER THIRTY-ONE

Sam stood in the middle of the street, and he heard the scream.

It was a man. Quite clearly a man. Which meant it wasn't Tara. He hated that *that* was the first thing he thought when he heard the scream. But when you'd spent the last month searching for someone, yeah, that shit could really do a number on you.

He stood in the middle of the street. Looked around at the buildings around him. Upon thinking, it didn't sound like it was coming from one of those. It sounded like it was coming from the woods beyond the buildings, which made Sam feel even more uncertain. Even more unsure. Something wasn't right. Something wasn't right at all.

Sam looked around at Seann. Saw him standing there, staring, wide-eyed. "We need—we need to see who it is," Seann said.

Sam shook his head. "Absolutely not."

"So we're supposed to just leave someone screaming out there?"

"Yes. That's exactly what we're going to do."

"What the fuck happened to your humanity?"

"The blackout happened. The last fucking *year* happened. That's what happened. And have you literally learned nothing about this world and how to survive in it?"

"I've learned not to leave people behind," Seann said. "I've learned not to give up on people. And I've learned that when people are in danger—when they need help—we can't just abandon them. We—we just can't."

Sam shook his head. He couldn't actually believe that after all the gains made in their friendship, they were bickering about this shit right now. "Well, I'll let you have that moral debate of yours to yourself," Sam said. "But right now, I'm walking. I'm not mad keen on this storm. We need to keep walking."

He started walking. Heard that scream again. It was so loud. So piercing. Whoever it was sounded in agony. Sounded in a lot of pain. And he felt guilty about walking on. He really did. That wasn't a lie. He didn't like leaving people behind. Didn't like leaving *anyone* behind. Seann was ruthless to suggest there was anything about this that he liked at all. That was way off the mark.

But... there were more important matters at hand. More pressing matters at hand. If you started worrying about every single person who needed help in this world, you'd really never get anywhere at all.

He kept on walking when he noticed something.

Seann. He couldn't hear his footsteps right beside him. He couldn't hear him at all.

Sam stopped. Turned around.

Seann was standing there. Right where he'd stood before. He hadn't moved a muscle.

Sam stopped. Rolled his eyes. "Seann. I get it. But—"

"I know you get it," Seann said. "Deep down, I know you get it. I know walking away from people isn't you. I know leaving people behind isn't you. But—but we were all this man once. We've all been there. We've all needed help at some point. And you're telling me we're supposed to just walk away? You're telling me we're supposed to just leave this man behind?"

"You're being fucking stupid."

"Maybe I am. But if I'm stupid for having hope, is that so bad?"

Sam shook his head. Now really wasn't the time for this naive bullcrap. "We don't know it's not a trap."

"Chances are, it isn't a trap."

"But there's a chance it is a trap. And we're the only people alive who might be able to help Tara right now."

"At what cost?" Seann asked.

Sam stood there. He waited for Seann to join him. Waited for him to walk towards him. For his resolve to break as that screaming continued.

"I'm sorry," Seann said. "But—but you have your demons, and I have mine. And I... I'm not leaving this man, Sam. I'm not leaving him. I'm sorry."

And then he turned around. Walked down by the sides of the house towards the trees. Disappeared.

Sam stood there. Stood there in the middle of the road. The wind blew against him. Rain drizzled onto him. And as he stood there in the silence, he felt... he felt alone. He felt truly alone.

Seann was gone. Seann had walked away. Just like that, he was gone, and Sam was on his own. He couldn't believe his stupidity. His naivety. If he were watching this play out on screen right now, he'd be screaming at Seann to come right the hell back.

"Well," Sam said, turning around shaking his head. "Suit yourself."

He walked down the road. Walked into the wind. Into the rain. And the more he walked, the more he tried to tell himself that he was doing the right thing. He tried to tell himself that Seann was the one blinded by whatever shit he had going on. And that he was being careless. Reckless.

But the more he walked... the more something else started to happen. The more he walked, the more he began to realise that he wasn't in the right. That he couldn't just leave Seann. The more he walked, the more he realised just how much Seann had sacrificed for him—just how much he'd given up for him. And now he was just walking away from him? Now he was walking away from him at the first sign of trouble?

Sam stopped. He looked back. Heard that scream again. The scream that made the hairs on the back of his neck stand on end. Because hearing that scream... it made him think of Seann. It made him think of the guilt he'd feel if he abandoned Seann and lost Seann, all in the name of finding Tara.

And the longer he stood there, the more he realised he couldn't just leave Seann. He couldn't just abandon him. He couldn't just walk away from him.

"Fuck it," Sam said. "Can't actually believe I'm doing this. Might just be the most stupid fucking thing I've ever done. But screw it."

He started walking back towards where Seann had disappeared when he saw something.

Right there, on the back of a road sign. Those three letters. He'd missed them. Walked right past them. Because they were on the *back* of the sign he was heading towards.

But he could see them now. They were staring him right in the face.

NRS.

And then a few more letters right underneath.

New base. Five miles east. Safety.

Sam stood there. Shaking. His heart racing. His chest tight.

A new base? Five miles east? It almost seemed too good to be true in a way.

But what if?

What if?

"Seann," he shouted, walking down to the road where Seann had disappeared. Picking up the pace a little.

He kept walking. A little faster now.

"Seann!" he shouted. His voice echoing against the walls.

As he walked further down the alleyway beside the shops, staring at the trees behind them, two things dawned on Sam.

First, there was no sign of Seann.

And secondly?

That screaming. It'd stopped.

Sam stood there. Looking down the side of the shops. The wind howling. His heart racing. And everything so silent. Everything so damned *quiet*.

He gritted his teeth, and he walked down the alleyway, down by the sides of the shops. "Seann," he said. "Where you at?"

But the more Sam searched, the more Sam looked, the more Sam tried to find Seann, a horrible realisation began to settle in.

The realisation that he was already too late.

Wherever Seann was, he wasn't here.

Seann was gone.

CHAPTER THIRTY-TWO

Sam stepped into the woods and he knew this was a terrible fucking idea.

But he figured objectively, the entire last fucking *month* was a terrible idea. So he couldn't just leave Seann to die in that ditch right now.

The clouds were thick. The branches above suffocated the light from these woods, making it feel dark in here. The branches and the leaves didn't protect him from the rain either, which was falling down so damned heavily now. He felt lost. He felt disoriented. But more than anything, he felt guilty.

Because Seann was gone.

He paced through the muddy ground of the woods and tried to find a single trace of Seann. Seann had been stupid, wandering off in search of that scream like he had. He should've known better. Far, far better.

But then... what if it was partly on Sam? Maybe Sam shouldn't have let him walk off alone. Maybe Sam should've gone after him. Maybe he should've stood beside him, and maybe they should've approached this together.

Because right now, only one thing was true.

Seann was gone. Seann was gone, and the screaming had stopped.

Which meant... well. Sam didn't know *what* it meant. But it wasn't good. It couldn't be good. Unless Seann had found the screaming bloke. Unless he'd found him, and he was okay, and there was nothing to worry about at all.

But that didn't seem likely, somehow. It didn't seem likely at all.

More likely?

Something had happened to Seann. Seann was in danger.

And it didn't matter whose fucking fault it was that he was in danger... Sam couldn't just walk away from him.

He thought back to that sign as he paced through the woods, squinting everywhere for a sign of movement, a sign of life. The sign painted with the NRS logo. With those words underneath it. *New base. Five miles east. Safety.* And he felt so uncertain about it. He felt like it was so fucking *off* it was unbelievable.

And yet he was looking past everything his gut feeling was screaming at him. Because of Tara. Because of the letter he'd found. He was ignoring all the signs of danger and chaos all because of the note he had found. And didn't that make him so fucking stupid, really?

Because there was someone here with him. There was a man who had given up everything to help him. And he hadn't appreciated that. He hadn't shown enough gratitude. He hadn't shown enough appreciation. Nowhere near enough.

And now that man was gone.

He kept on walking. Heart pounding. He wasn't sure how much longer he could search or how much more there was to see. Only that Seann couldn't have got too far. He wasn't far ahead of him at all earlier. He didn't even look like he was running when Sam saw him disappear down the side of the shops. So where the fuck was he? Where the fuck had he gone?

He looked around, completely lost, completely disoriented,

completely trapped in the clutches of the woods, when he noticed something.

Two footprints.

Two footprints, right there in the mud, staring up at him.

Sam walked over to them slowly. Saw them right there, staring up at him. He tried to follow them with his gaze. Tried to see some more ahead of these.

But there was nothing. Not a mark. Not a single trace.

He looked at those two prints. Saw which direction they were heading in. Saw they were heading straight on. And as much as he felt unsure about this, as much as he felt a serious sense of unease about this... he knew he had to follow them. He knew he had to keep going. He knew Seann's life might depend on it.

He looked up into the darkness where Seann had disappeared when he saw something.

Movement.

Definite movement, right there. Right ahead in the woods.

Sam stood still. Very fucking still. 'Cause he'd seen someone. He'd seen someone move in there. And it made him feel uneasy. It made him feel... unsafe.

He lifted his rifle. Pointed it ahead. Needed to be careful. If Seann came wandering out, and he accidentally shot Seann... fuck, he didn't want to think about it. Didn't want to even consider it.

But if there was someone else... someone who posed a threat. Someone who could put him in danger... then he needed to be on guard. He needed to be ready.

He walked slowly through the woods. Rifle pointed. Squinting right ahead. His heart raced. His chest was tight. He swore he kept seeing movement in his eyes. Colours in his vision lighting up the darkness.

But the more he stood there, the more he looked, the more he realised he was probably just imagining things. It was probably all just in his head.

Probably.

He swallowed a lump in his throat. Tightened his grip around the rifle. He didn't know what he was going to find in these woods. He didn't know what he was going to come across. But the thoughts haunted him. Plagued him.

The thought of finding Seann. Dead. Staring up at him with blood trickling out of his head.

Or of Tara...

He thought about Tara, and he thought about Seann, and then he thought about Rebecca, and Leonard, and Harvey, and Claude and Marky. He didn't even know where they were. He didn't know where they'd gone. He couldn't even be sure they were safe.

He just had to hope.

He just had to pray.

He took another step into that darkness, towards the exact spot he'd seen that movement, when suddenly he felt something.

It all happened so fast.

A tightness. A tightness around his right ankle.

Fuck. What...

He looked down, and before he had time to properly register what was happening, he felt himself flying up towards the trees above.

He felt the rifle tumbling out of his hand.

"Fuck!" Sam shouted. A trap. A fucking trap. Of course, it was a fucking trap.

He dangled there. Dangled from his ankle. Tried to look around. Tried to get his bearings. Tried to see. Completely disoriented.

"Seann!" Sam shouted. Because it was all he could think of shouting. "Where are you? 'Cause... cause I could really do with a fucking hand right now. I could really..."

And then it all happened so quickly.

Someone spun him around.

Put a finger in front of their lips.

And then they pulled back a baton in their hands and cracked him right across the skull.

CHAPTER THIRTY-THREE

Sam opened his eyes, and as disoriented as he felt, he was sure of one thing.

He was screwed.

It was dark and cloudy. He was cold, and he was wet. He was in the middle of the woods, by the looks of things. And he was upside-down. Damn, where was he? And what'd happened for him to end up here?

He squinted around the darkness. Squinted through the trees. He could hear something—ringing in his ears. And something else, too. Something that sounded like... like footsteps.

Footsteps. Getting closer. Somewhere behind him.

And then suddenly, it dawned on him as he dangled there, the taste of blood filling his mouth.

He'd gone searching for Seann. Followed him into the woods. Tried to find him and tried to find the source of that scream. Only... Fuck. He'd stepped on something, and it'd dragged him up into the air, and now here he was, dangling from a rope. The taste of blood in his mouth. Ears ringing. And his head aching like mad.

He tried to turn around. Tried to look towards that approaching figure. He didn't know who it was or what they wanted, but he figured he didn't have to know much, really, did he? They were a lunatic. They were a nutter. The world was full of them. Completely fucking full of them.

He tried to turn around, his body shaking, his head so heavy as he dangled upside-down, so disoriented and dizzy.

And then he saw something else.

Or rather, some*one* else.

Up ahead, dangling from another tree not far away from him, he saw Seann. Seann was dangling just like he was. His nose was bleeding, and the blood was trickling down to the forest floor below. And Sam wanted to feel annoyed at him. He wanted to be fucking fuming at this prick for walking them both right into this trap. He knew it was a fucking trap. The second he'd heard the bloody screaming, he knew it was a bloody trap. But he'd followed him anyway. He'd followed him, and now here he was. And while he was dangling here like a fucking dickhead, Tara was out there somewhere, still in danger. In deep, deep danger.

But at the same time... Seann was only trying to do the right thing. That bastard was only trying to do the right thing. So he couldn't hate him for it. As much as he wanted to, he couldn't hate him for it.

He went to shout out for Seann to get his attention when suddenly he felt something either side of him.

Two hands, spinning him round. Spinning him around so he was faced with his captor.

It was an old man. Bearded. Bleary-eyed. Looked hard as nails. Old, but tough.

"The fuck are you doing in my woods?" the man asked.

Sam narrowed his eyes. "I mean, you've not really given us much of a fucking choice—"

"Don't fuck with me," the man shouted. And that's when Sam realised he was holding a rifle. One of Sam's or Seann's rifles. Pointing it right at him. "Answer. Wandering around my town. And in my woods. You one of those NRS cunts?"

NRS. Did this bloke know about the NRS? "What—what do you know about them?"

The man swung the butt of the rifle against Sam's face, hard, and he felt his nose crack upon impact. "Fuck," Sam said.

"Here's how it's gonna go," the man said. "I ask the questions. You answer. For every question you don't answer or answer with some smart-arse remark, I hurt you. And if you *keep* on chatting back, I hurt your friend here. You understand?"

Sam glared over at Seann as he hung there from that tree. Judging by the state of his face, he'd already been through a rough time of it. "My friend here has a lot to answer for, getting us into this fucking mess in the first place—"

Another crack, right across Sam's face.

"Okay," Sam said, wincing. "Okay. We... we were heading north."

"Heading north where?"

"The NRS. We—"

"Are you NRS?"

"Do we *look* NRS?"

"I don't know. But I don't like those fuckers. And I don't trust two blokes who appear in the middle of nowhere pretending they're here by mistake or whatever. So—so you'd better start talking."

Sam sighed. As much as he wanted to be awkward with this guy, he could see he wasn't just any old lunatic. He was worried. Paranoid, even. But he knew something about the NRS. And for that reason, he might be able to help.

And, besides. He kind of had them dangling from a tree right now. So he was kind of in the position of power.

"Look," Sam said.

"I'm looking very fucking closely, and I don't like what I see." He pulled his rifle back. Went to swing it at Sam again.

"We're just trying—trying to find someone," Sam said before the man had a chance to whack him again. "My... my friend. Tara.

She's... she's in danger. She's with a man. A man who... a man who I don't trust."

"Jealous lover, are you?" the bloke said.

"No—"

"Something like that," Seann shouted.

Sam frowned. The fuck? This bastard was meant to be on his side.

"I... We were walking through the town. I wanted to keep walking. My friend here heard the scream. Which I'm assuming was you, by the way."

The man nodded. "Got a talent for it."

Sam resisted the urge to tell him he had an uncanny resemblance to a teenage girl when he screamed. He really didn't fancy another whack across the face right now.

He wanted to stand up for himself. He wanted to tell this bastard where to shove it. But at the same time, Sam saw Seann dangling from the rope. He saw himself dangling from the rope. And he remembered what Seann told him. About how pissed off with him he'd been for what happened back at the arena. For the trouble his stubbornness and his attitude had got them both in. And he realised right now there was nothing to be gained from attitude.

"We're sorry," Sam said. "We... we really are just passing through. You let us go. You let us walk. And—and I swear we won't bother you again. Well... we'll be gone. Just like that. Right out of your way."

The man stared at Sam. Narrow-eyed. Holding that rifle and pointing it right at him.

And for a moment, for just a moment, Sam thought he might've got through to him. He thought he might've won him over. He thought he might've actually made this man see sense.

But then the man took a deep breath. Sighed.

"You see, I'm not sure I believe you," he said.

And then he pulled out a knife and swung it right at Sam.

CHAPTER THIRTY-FOUR

Sam watched the knife fly towards him, and not for the first fucking time in his life, as he dangled upside down from that tree, he was pretty convinced he was going to die.

Only he didn't die. Of course he didn't fucking die.

That knife. It missed Sam. Missed him completely. And even though Sam held his breath and braced for the inevitable pain... he didn't feel anything. He didn't feel anything at all.

Not until he noticed he was falling.

And just like that, he slammed against the ground. Face flat. Splatted right in some mud.

He lay there. Turned around. His face hurt. His neck ached. His back ached. Fuck, he was sore.

But... but he was free.

For now, he was free.

He rolled around onto his back when he saw the man staring down at him.

He wasn't pointing the rifle at him. Not anymore. He was just standing there. Standing over him. Staring down at him with big, wide eyes.

And Sam didn't know what this was. He didn't know what was happening. He didn't know what this guy's deal was. He just knew that he needed to be careful. He needed to play this right. 'Cause the guy might've cut him down, but that didn't mean he was out of the woods just yet—figuratively or literally. Not at all.

He had to have his guard up. He had to be careful. And he had to watch out. No matter what.

And then, out of nowhere, the man held out a hand. "Come on."

Sam stared at it. Still a little fucking baffled and surprised, in all truth. "You—you what?"

"Get up," he said. "Unless you want to stay lying there on the ground all afternoon. And if you do... well, be my fucking guest, I guess?"

Sam lay there. Staring at this man's hand. Then shaking his head. "I..."

"Look," the man said. "I know you're not NRS. The way I see it, if you were NRS or anyone who knew about me for that matter, you wouldn't be dumb enough to stumble along here. You can't know about me. Or you'd stay far, far away from me."

Sam held his breath. Winced a little. Shit this guy really was a tough motherfucker. "Who... who are you?"

"Like I said. We can all have this conversation in my cabin. Or you can stay out here in the rain, and this goes nowhere. I know which I'd rather. So choose carefully."

Sam shook his head. To be honest, he still couldn't quite believe he was actually alive. He was fully expecting to be stabbed in the guts or shot in the head just a moment ago. And now here he was. Being offered some kind of shelter by a guy who'd caught him in a trap. What were the chances?

"Get up," the man said. "Get some shelter. Have some food. And then you can be on your way. But you need to be careful around here. Trust me. Before you go wandering any further like this... you need to be very careful."

"What do you know?"

The man sighed. "How many bloody times do I have to tell you? I'm not having this conversation here. We go inside. Or you stay here. And good luck to you. Really. But I don't fancy your chances. And you'd be a fool to fancy yours. So come on. On your damned feet. If you've got any sense about you. And honestly, I'm starting to wonder."

Sam didn't trust this bastard. But he also wasn't keen on staying lying down here. And this bloke, he sounded like he knew what he was talking about. He knew this place. And he knew shit about the NRS. And as much as Sam would much rather just keep walking right now because time was running out... he found himself falling more into Seann's mindset. A mindset of not being rash. Of weighing up their options. And of gathering all the information they possibly could before moving on.

He looked over at Seann. Dangling there. Seann shook his head. Almost like he was expecting Sam to turn this man down.

Well, Seann. You're in for a fucking shocker.

"Okay," Sam said.

Seann looked around. Wide-eyed.

Sam grabbed the man's hand. He stood up. Brushed a bit of the dirt off his back. And the man looked right at him through narrowed eyes. Really studying him. Really weighing him up as he stood there, all dizzy and disoriented.

"Well?" Sam said. "I thought you didn't want to stand out here in the rain?"

The man nodded. Grunted. "Come on." And then he started walking off through the woods, over to the left.

"What about my friend?" Sam asked.

"Yeah," Seann shouted. "Don't—don't just leave me. What about—what about me?"

"You said it was him who got you caught here?" the man asked.

Sam nodded. "Something like that."

"Well why don't we leave him here to think on his stupidity for a while?"

Sam smirked. He smirked at the sight of Seann's face turning. He smirked as he saw him kicking out, trying aimlessly to break free. "Don't leave me, you shits. Don't you dare fucking leave me! Sam!"

"Just long enough to worry him," Sam said.

"That sounds about right to me."

And as Seann dangled there, shouting out for help, Sam had to admit something he never thought he'd ever admit again.

He actually quite liked this stranger.

CHAPTER THIRTY-FIVE

Sam sat in the stranger's cabin, and as much as he wanted to get moving, he had to admit it was quite a luxury to enjoy the company of a man who, firstly, wasn't Seann and, secondly, wasn't a complete and utter lunatic.

The stranger wasn't so much of a stranger anymore. He was called Dave. And they hadn't left Seann tied up outside. They'd cut him down soon enough. A bit of a practical joke, which Seann didn't see too much of a funny side to. And yeah, Sam accepted it was a bit of a dick move. But joking about and messing around... it was few and far between these days. Even if it was at someone else's expense, Sam had to admit it was quite funny.

Anyway, Seann seemed to have stopped sulking about it. They were inside this cabin. Sitting around an open fireplace. It felt so warm. So comforting. Sitting there, listening to the crackling of the logs, the smell of the burning wood filling his lungs. He had a cold glass of water in hand. Felt like the freshest glass of water he'd had in a lifetime. And his belly was full, too. Rabbit stew. And an absolutely delicious rabbit stew at that.

Yeah. This guy, Dave, he seemed alright.

But the longer Sam sat here, the more he got comfortable, the more his guilt grew. Because he shouldn't be in here, sitting in front of a fire, enjoying any luxuries. He should be out there. Searching for Tara. Searching for Kurt. Searching for the NRS, whoever they were.

But this guy. Dave. He'd mentioned the NRS. Said he knew who they were. Didn't seem to like them all that much. And if he knew something about the NRS, that meant he might be able to help him find Tara.

Sam looked over at this man. He was old. Bearded. He didn't look like the sort of guy who smiled much. This cabin was pretty barebones, but there were a few photo frames in here. Photographs sitting on the mantlepiece of the fire. This man in years gone by. And a little girl beside him, smiling widely.

"So what do you know about the NRS?" Sam asked.

The man sighed. "I know they're not the sort of folks you want to run into."

"Can you be more specific?"

The man shrugged. "I mean, is *any* large group the kind of folks you want to run into, really?"

Sam really studied this man. He could hear what he was saying. Where there were large groups, there was trouble. There were power hierarchies. There were struggles. As far as Sam was concerned, these bigger groups were always a recipe for disaster. They never lasted. Ever.

"So you don't really know a thing about them, is what you're saying?" Sam asked.

"I'm saying I've seen enough of people in this world to know it's better not to fuck with 'um."

"And what makes us different?" Sam asked.

It was a question that seemed to stump Dave. A question that stopped him in his tracks. He looked down at the fire. Wide-eyed. And Sam swore he saw a wateriness in those old eyes of his. Eyes that had seen so much. An unexpected vulnerability hidden beneath all the layers of that onion.

"It gets... it gets lonely sometimes. Since I lost... Since Maria went away."

Sam felt a knot in his throat. Because that's what it was always about, wasn't it? Loss always had this effect on him. It was something he could relate to. The pain of loss—however it happened, and whoever it was—was enough for him not to want to love again. Not to want to experience connection again. Because when connection was always coupled with the risk of loss—which it always was by its very nature, wasn't it?—it hardly felt worth it.

But seeing this man sitting right here, seeing the look on his face, seeing the pain in his eyes... Sam had a very different reaction to the one he usually had. A very different reaction to the one he expected.

"So that's it?" Sam asked.

Dave turned around. Frowned. "What?"

"I just... I dunno. I used to... I used to think like you do. But now I... I don't know. I'm starting to think it's worth it. Connection. Even... even when there's a risk it all goes away."

Dave stared at him. And Seann stared at him too. Which kind of bugged him a bit because he'd said exactly the sort of thing Seann had been trying to convince him of for days now.

Dave sat there for a few seconds. A few seconds that felt like they dragged on forever. And then he took a deep breath, and he sighed. "You rest up as long as you need to. And then you move on from this place. And you don't tell anyone about this place or that you've been here."

Sam's stomach sank. Because he could see from the look in this man's eyes that he was just terrified. He wanted company. He was desperately lonely. But at the same time... he was just so terrified. He was just so afraid. Not of other people. Not of anything bad happening to him or anything like that.

He was terrified of loss.

And as Sam sat here... he kind of saw a mirror image of himself staring back at him. A vision from the future. The kind of man he could end up if he kept on pushing people away. Or if he kept on going down the road he was going down. The road of pushing everyone else other than Tara away. Especially when, as painful as it was to admit, there was no way of knowing if she was still even out there.

He had to open himself to the possibility that he would never find her again. And he had to ask himself whether this man was really the sort of man he turned into in years to come.

He wanted to argue, and he wanted to protest. But in the end, Sam just nodded.

"We'll be out of your way in a couple of hours. But don't... don't lose hope."

"Don't lose hope in what?"

"In... in other people."

A smile stretched up Dave's face. He laughed a little. "Brother, I don't have any hope left to lose."

They sat there around the fire, silent. Watching the flames flickering in front of them. Feeling the relaxation seep through their bones.

And as much as Sam knew this moment couldn't last forever— as much as none of them knew this moment could last forever— right here, Sam felt a sense of connection that was so, so rare in this world.

A moment of connection that, like the flames and like everything else, would soon disappear into darkness.

CHAPTER THIRTY-SIX

S am and Seann waited for sunrise before setting off on their journey once again.

It was a nice morning. Really pleasant. There were some days that, even knowing the context of the world you were living in—even knowing about the horrors that were being committed and the struggle that so many survivors were going through—you just couldn't help but stop and appreciate the beauty of the world around you. The sound of the birds singing in the sky. The cool breeze against your skin. The freshness of the air filling your lungs with woody, grassy scents. Sam had always been a fan of nature. He'd always felt more at home in nature than he had in towns and cities and just around other people in general. So in some ways, he'd found the post-electricity world *more* comfortable, in a primal kind of way. Sure, increased risks came with living in a world like this. The bigger threats of danger. But when things were good, and when they were calm... they were calm in a way that the world was never calm before. It was kind of comforting.

But there *was* always that reality hanging over him. There was always that reminder, cutting through the daydream of goodness.

And that reality was what he was doing. What his goal was. What his purpose was.

Finding Tara.

Finding Kurt.

Finding them wherever they were.

He looked around at Seann. He hadn't said much today. Not in a way that was awkward or anything like that. Quite the opposite. If anything, things just felt more *comfortable* between them. Things just felt more... natural.

And that encounter with Dave... it'd awoken something inside Sam. It'd changed something.

"You did a good thing back there," Seann said.

Sam raised an eyebrow. "Huh?"

"Dave. You... Well. Once upon a time, you'd've shot him before he had the chance to invite us back for supper."

Sam tilted his head. He was deeply sceptical of people who called dinner "supper". "I figured there was nothing threatening about him."

"I think it's probably more than that."

"Oh, I forgot. Armchair psychologist Seann is on the fucking case again."

"I'm just saying," Seann said. "I think... I think you're finally beginning to see, aren't you?"

Sam rolled his eyes. "See what?"

"What really matters."

He looked at Seann, and he hated how smug this bastard looked. And he hated how irritatingly *right* he was, too. As always. "Jesus," Sam said. "*Were* you some kind of therapist or something?"

"I was, actually. Well. Not really."

"That makes sense."

"What I mean is... it's the career I always wanted to take. It's the career I trained for. The career I went to uni for. But... but I had to drop out. Mum got sick. Had to pay the bills somehow. So

I... I quit uni and went home to help her. Spent my student grant on providing her as much care as I could. Lost all my friends. Didn't argue or anything. Just... well. When you're twenty-one, you want to be out partying and clubbing. Not hanging out with your mate and his mum. And I... I didn't want to leave her side. I couldn't bear the thought of her dying when I wasn't there. Even though she... Well. She was never the most supportive to me. But even so."

Sam gulped. "I'm sorry to hear that."

"In the end, it didn't matter. She took off, and she disappeared. They never... they never found her body. But presumed dead. Presumed suicide. Figure she washed out into the sea and never came back. But there... there was always that mystery, you know? That mystery of whether she was still out there. I like to think that sometimes. It makes... it makes everything I did to try and help her and comfort her seem less... pointless, somehow."

Sam didn't know what to say. He wasn't good at handling emotional situations like this. He wasn't a good therapist. And he was hearing out a man who had tried to become a therapist himself. So it was an interesting combination.

"So yeah. After that, hospitality, then minimum wage office jobs. No real progression. But the dream never died, you know? Colin was always... he was always encouraging like that."

Sam stood there, and he felt even fucking shittier about being a dick with Seann. There were so many layers to his past. So many tragedies he hadn't even considered before this point. So many losses. And considering them at all was painful, wasn't it? Considering them was acknowledging that other people hurt, too. That other people had their own shit going on. And sometimes... sometimes it was just easier to distance yourself from that shit.

"You were a dick for keeping me tied up that tree," Seann said.

"And you were a dick for dragging me there in the first place."

Seann rolled his eyes. "We've been through this. I wasn't just going to leave a screaming man to die."

"Well, hopefully, next time you hear a screaming fucking man in the woods, you won't be so melodramatic about it."

Seann shook his head. "If I hadn't, we would never have met Dave."

"For every Dave, there's ten Kurts."

"Is that really how you see the world?"

"Yes. It's the reason I'm still alive. And you should see the world that way, too. If you want to survive much longer."

"I'm alive because I *haven't* lost hope," Seann said. "And I... I just wish you could see the world the same way, too."

Sam stood there. Seann stood there. Both of them a lot closer than they were. But both caught in this weird conflict of morals and emotions about the most important things.

Sam went to say something when he saw Seann's eyes widen. And his first instinct was... fuck. There was someone here. They were in deep shit. There was someone here, and they were in trouble.

But Seann didn't raise his rifle.

Instead, he just pointed. Nodded into the distance.

Sam turned around. Unsure of whether he wanted to see whatever Seann was looking at or not. And when he first turned around, he wasn't sure what Seann was looking at. It wasn't some*one*. So what was it?

"What..." Sam started.

And then he saw it, right there on the wall opposite, impossible to miss.

On the wall opposite, he saw the graffiti.

That familiar white spray paint.

And on that wall, the words that sparked two emotions: hope and fear.

NRS.

One Mile.

Welcome home.

CHAPTER THIRTY-SEVEN

"How far did the sign say?"

"You know how far the sign said."

"Don't be cryptic. Just answer the damned question."

"Two miles."

"It didn't say two miles."

"Exactly, Sam. So you don't have to ask me how far the sign said."

"Just answer the bloody question, Seann. It said a mile, right?"

Seann nodded. "Yes. Yes, it said a mile."

"And we've been walking—"

"More than a mile. Yes."

"Which means..."

"We don't know what it means."

Sam sighed. Rubbed his fingers through his hair, which felt like it was getting thinner by the day. Damn, he *must* be stressed. He always used to pride himself on his hair and how thick it was. It was something Rebecca used to like about him.

And just thinking of Rebecca... it made his stomach turn. He'd been so hyperfocused on finding Tara that he hadn't taken all that much time to even consider Rebecca and Leonard.

Wherever they were, he hoped they were okay. That was a worry for another time.

Right now, he was fucking worried enough about finding this NRS place. And it wasn't going well. It wasn't going well at all.

They'd been walking further than a mile, and they hadn't seen a thing. A few empty towns and villages. But mostly just roads. Empty roads. And the further Sam and Seann walked, the more Sam began to worry. What if he'd got this wrong? What if this was a trap? What if he'd been ignoring the clear red flags all along, all because he was so focused on finding Tara?

Because he'd grilled Seann for walking off into the woods and getting them both captured when he'd heard the screaming yesterday. But how was what *he* was doing any different at all, really? What made this entire naive search any different?

"Just chill, Sam," Seann said.

"Chill? That's your answer? Really?"

"I'm just... It said a mile. It might not be exactly a mile."

"It said a mile."

"You think they dragged a tape measure along or something?"

"I just... It said a mile. And I haven't... I haven't seen a trace. Of anything. And neither have you. What if... what if we've got this wrong?"

Seann shrugged. Which seemed like a rather dismissive way of reacting to Sam raising a possibility that he'd feared all along but been too afraid to vocalise. "I mean, it's always been a possibility, hasn't it?"

Sam shook his head. "Her letter. It said—"

"Her letter said they were heading north. To the NRS. We have no idea whether they were following different signs. We have no idea if she already found them and... and disappeared with them. We've got nothing but a hunch, Sam. You know that.

You've always known that, deep down. It's about time you finally started accepting it. Properly."

Sam wanted to argue. Quite frankly, he wanted to tell Seann to piss off with his negativity. But he couldn't. Because he was right, wasn't he? As much as he hated to admit it, Seann was right. It wasn't pleasant to face. It wasn't nice to admit. But he was right.

"I warned you about this," Seann said as they continued to pace down the road towards the trees in the distance."

"Warned me about what?"

"About the risks. Of putting your faith into one outcome. Because if... if that's not the outcome you end up with, then you're stuck, aren't you? You're—you're completely back to square one."

Sam shook his head. He didn't want to hear this shit right now. He knew it was true. He knew Seann was right, and he had a point. But... but he just still didn't want to hear it.

"We keep walking," Sam said.

"And when we walk another mile? And another mile? What then?"

"What do you suggest?"

"I don't know what I suggest," Seann shouted. "I just... I just don't know how much further we can go like this. Not you. Not me. *We.* Because this road... I don't see it ending, Sam. I don't see it ending well. That's—that's the honest truth. That's me levelling with you. And I just worry that if you don't get the ending to this journey you want... I just worry about what might be next."

Again, Sam heard Seann loud and clear. And again, he understood. He got what he was saying. He got what he was saying completely.

But hearing right now... it was painful, and it was raw, and it was not what he wanted to hear.

"We keep going," Sam said. Because it was all he could say. "Like... like you said. It might be more than a mile."

Seann opened his mouth like he was going to protest. Then he sighed. Nodded. "It might be more than a mile."

They walked further. Further down this road. Further towards the trees in the distance. And as they walked, Sam felt his hope dwindling. He felt the reality settling in. And the reality was that they were not going to find any NRS camp. They were not going to find Tara. And they were not going to find Kurt. This was their life now. And it was a life Sam was going to have to adapt to.

He walked further down the road when he noticed something up ahead.

Through the trees. Through the trees, just up ahead. He could see something. Something down a hill. Something off in the distance.

"Sam?" Seann said.

But Sam wasn't listening. He walked. He walked down the road. And then he started jogging down the road past the abandoned cars.

"Sam!" Seann shouted.

But Sam wasn't hearing him. He wasn't listening. Because he could only see what was in the distance. He could only glimpse what was behind the trees.

And he could only wonder if... well, what if?

What if this was what he thought it was?

He ran further down the road. All sense of danger out the window. All reservations and all sense of caution gone. Ignoring Seann, as he called for him, as he told him to be careful, as he told him to stop.

But as Sam kept on running, he started to see.

He started to see it.

And he felt the smile creep across his face.

He felt the relief hit his body.

And he felt the weight rise right off his shoulders.

He stopped. Looked down the slope. Looked right down the road. Heart racing. Breathing heavily. Smiling.

"Sam?" Seann said. "What..."

And then he stopped.

He stopped, and he laughed.

And he looked at Sam, and Sam laughed, too.

"Fuck," Seann said. "It's... it's it. It's—it's actually it."

Sam looked back around at what was in front of him, right in the distance. And as he looked down the slope into the morning sun, he couldn't help smiling.

Because in the distance, Sam could see a community.

He could see a town.

He could see the walls around it. And he could see the letters, smeared right across one of those entrances, right down the hill.

NRS.

Welcome Home.

They'd made it.

This was it.

They were here.

CHAPTER THIRTY-EIGHT

Tara saw the sign up ahead and felt a shiver creep down her spine.

NRS.

Welcome home.

It was morning, and it was cloudy. She felt a little shivery anyway, in all truth. Didn't know if it was the weather or if she was coming down with something. It wouldn't surprise her. She'd been walking for God knows how long. And before that, she'd been tied up in Kurt's hellhole. Fuck, maybe dying on the spot of sickness wouldn't be such a bad way to go after all. Certainly seemed the better alternative to travelling any further with Kurt.

Kurt smiled when he saw the sign. Laughed a little. Not in a menacing, comic book villain kind of way. More... well, an authentic kind of way. Like he was genuinely surprised. Genuinely happy. "We're almost there. We've—we've almost made it."

She looked at Kurt and saw that smile, and she still couldn't get her head around this guy. She'd learned about this weird duality to him these last days and weeks they'd been travelling. Because he was a monster. No doubt about that. He was a psychopathic monster with a god complex and no real shred of empathy for anyone but himself.

But there was also something... well, strangely tragic about him. She didn't know a lot about him. Only the facade he presented to the world. But underneath that facade, in moments of silence and quiet, it was strange. Because she saw a kid. A lost kid who truly believed that maybe, just maybe, his life could get better. But who kept on realising that no matter how far he went down the road of *trying* to be a better person... he was still the same monster underneath. You couldn't change human nature. You could try to be better. You could try to be different. But at your core—at your very, deepest core—you could not change who you were.

"You've done well," Kurt said. "Making it this far. I'm—I'm quite impressed."

"And I'm looking forward to getting there and telling these people how much of a piece of shit you are."

Kurt rolled his eyes. "You're still assuming you're going to make it there, then?"

"Why would you bring me this far just to kill me now?"

"Don't tempt me," Kurt said.

But he stared at her when he'd said those words. Stared at her again in a way that made her feel... well, strangely uncomfortable. Because it was like he was *flirting* with her. It was like, in his own weird way, he was trying to bridge some sort of bond between them. Like she was some sort of... experiment for him. And it was weird. It was really fucking weird. But it was something she wanted to ask him about.

"So you've kept me around this long," Tara said.

"I have."

"And if you're planning on murdering me some time soon—"

"A possibility."

"Right. But I... I guess I just want to know what... Fuck, what drives you? To do what you do? To be who you are? You've kidnapped me. You've abducted me. And you've kept me alive this long. I figure I... I dunno. If you're not intending to keep me around anyway, what harm is there in opening up a little?"

Kurt's eyes narrowed. It was like she'd just kicked his dog or something. Although, no. Bad analogy, 'cause Kurt was definitely the sort of motherfucker who found animal cruelty hilarious.

He looked off into the distance. Down the road. Over towards the trees and off towards that place where he no doubt pictured that one-mile sign pointed. "I... My whole life, people doubted me. My whole life, I felt like... I felt like I was different. Not that I wasn't good enough. But just... that I wasn't quite of this world. That I was different. Since... since the power went out, I've felt like I can be more myself. I've felt I can achieve things I've always wanted to achieve. I've... I've done horrible things. Cruel things. And now... now I've seen what it's like to have everything and lose everything again. And really it's... it's made me realise that there's just this emptiness. There's just this void inside all of us, isn't there? And I'm not sure how I fill that void. I'm not sure if I'll ever blend in. I'm not sure if I'll ever cure my own sickness. And I'm not sure if I ever want to. But I want to try. I want an opportunity to try."

He looked right at Tara then.

"And you've... you've made me realise that."

He stared at her, and she felt a shiver creep up her spine. "And how's that?"

"Because I know you feel the same."

She looked back at him now, and she felt something. Just for a moment, she felt something. A glimmer of truth to what he was saying. Because take away the monster he was and take away every fucking awful thing he'd done, and deep down, underneath everything... he was just trying to make his way in the world. Just like she was.

But he *was* a monster. And he'd done some horrible, horrible things. And he was going to pay for them. She was going to make sure of that.

"Maybe I won't kill you," Kurt said. "Maybe… maybe there can be another way. But I feel like if I keep you alive, if I loosen my grip… it's only me who will suffer for it. So you understand my predicament here."

Tara swallowed a lump in her throat. She nodded. And as much as she detested this animal, she couldn't help smiling at his wry sense of humour—at his way of bringing dark humour to the most horrible of topics: her own fucking death.

"You got that right," Tara said. "It is you who'll suffer for it. So you'd best keep a tight grip."

Kurt smiled. "I intend to."

He turned back to the road ahead. Looked down that road towards the clouds in the distance. And for a second, just a second, Tara saw that glimmer of humanity across his face again.

"Come on," he said. "We're almost there."

She watched him begin to walk down this road as they approached the NRS, and she took a deep breath of her own.

And then she took a step.

A step that she knew damn well might be one of her last.

CHAPTER THIRTY-NINE

Sam walked down the road towards the town that had to be the NRS base, and he wasn't sure what to think.

The place was bordered by metal fencing. Sam could see right through it, about ten feet high. There was barbed wire wrapped around the top of it. Just inside the confines of the base, he could see a few watchtowers. But he couldn't see anyone in there. No snipers. Nobody.

The road was quiet. All he could hear was his own footsteps and Seann's footsteps right beside him. That, and crows, cawing. The echoes of those caws filling the silence.

The air smelled smoky, somehow. A real harshness to the air clinging to his nostrils as he inhaled. It was like something had been burning here. Recently. And Sam dreaded to think what it might be. He couldn't even entertain the possibility that was circling his mind, like those crows circling above.

The gates to the community looked solid. Large metal sheets, two of them pushed up against one another. More than enough to keep outsiders out. The letters NRS sprayed across each of them.

Only there was a problem.

The gates were open.

Sam stood there. Stared beyond those open gates and into the community beyond. Inside, he could see empty streets. He could see blocks of flats, the windows smashed. He could see trees, and he could see the grey skies above.

But he couldn't see any movement. And he couldn't see any life.

He looked around at Seann. Seann looked back at him. He looked like he was going to say something. Like he was going to make one of his smartarse comments, which Sam really didn't frigging appreciate right now.

So Sam turned around again, and he walked towards this community. Rifle in hand. Not saying a word. Just knowing there had to be something here. There had to be some sign of the NRS here. There had to be some sign of *Tara* here. Because if there wasn't... what then?

"Sam," Seann said, finally breaking the silence.

Sam ignored him. Lifted his rifle and walked towards those open gates. He tried to focus ahead. Tried to look out for any movement. 'Cause there was an honest explanation for this. There *had* to be an honest explanation for this. The people here— the NRS, or whoever they were. They were in hiding. Or this was some kind of... some kind of trap. That's right. It was some kind of trap, and they'd seen Sam and Seann coming from miles away, and they were gonna appear out of nowhere and... and, well, and then what?

Sam's heart raced as he walked towards the darkness of the gates. That smell of burning grew stronger. There was a taste in his mouth, too. A sickly taste. He wasn't sure whether it was from the outside or from inside. But right now, he felt sick. He felt really fucking sick. And he couldn't shake that feeling.

"Sam," Seann said. "We need... we need to be careful."

But Sam wasn't listening. He was past listening to Seann. He was past listening to anyone.

So he kept on walking. Through those NRS-sprayed gates,

which were ajar. Because there had to be someone in here. There had to be someone in here, past those letters. Because this was where Tara was. This—this was where he'd been following a path to all along. And if there was nothing here...

No. He couldn't think like that. He just couldn't.

He stood in the entrance area to this community. Saw the empty road stretching up ahead. He heard those crows cawing louder right above. He felt the breeze against his skin. The specks of rain, cold against his face. And as he stood there, staring at the empty roads, staring at the darkened windows of the empty blocks of flats, that painful sense of inevitability started to weigh down on his shoulders. A reality he had been trying to run from. A possibility that he'd tried to avoid even considering. But a possibility that was now staring him right in the face.

"Sam," Seann said.

Sam walked on down this empty street. "They—they have to be there."

"Sam," Seann said. "This place, it's—"

"We can't just fucking give up. Not after... not after how far we've come."

But he could see the look on Seann's face. His eyes were wide. He looked like a parent breaking some bad news to a kid. A dead dog. A dead grandma. The sort of face they pulled when they realised their kid wasn't gonna understand it, wasn't gonna be able to comprehend it, but there was nothing they could do to change the outcome anyway.

"We can't give up," Sam said. "There has to be something. There—there has to be someone."

He turned. Carried on walking. And then his walk turned into a run. They had to be here. The NRS had to be here. Tara had to be here. This journey, it can't have been pointless. It can't have been for nothing.

Could it?

"Sam!" Seann shouted.

But Sam wasn't listening to him. He was done listening to him. He was only listening to himself. And right now, his only option was to keep on searching. To keep on looking. 'Cause he couldn't give up. He couldn't just give up.

He ran down the street. Kept on seeing movement in the corners of his eyes. But it was just the crows. Or the floaters that'd always plagued his vision. No sign of life. No sign of *her*.

He went to take a turn onto the next street when he saw something right up ahead.

He didn't know what it was. Not at first. A large mound right in the middle of the road. That's all he could see.

But then he smelled the burning.

He tasted the rot in the air.

And he heard the mass of flies buzzing around that mound.

He stood there.

Staring into the distance.

Trying to wrap his head around what he was looking at.

Trying to understand.

But the more he stood there, the more he stared... the more the pain inside him grew.

The more that fear took over.

The fear that his *worst* fears were wrong, all along.

Because right in front of him, Sam saw a huge mound of dead bodies.

Burned dead bodies.

And as he stood there, another reality hit him square in the face.

The reality that whoever was here—NRS or otherwise—they were not here anymore.

This place was empty.

The safe haven they'd spent so long searching for was empty.

The NRS were gone.

And so, too, was Sam's only lead on Tara.

CHAPTER FORTY

Sam stared at the pile of burned bodies in front of him and couldn't move a muscle.

The rain was falling quite heavily now. That smell in the air that always followed rain in warm weather. An earthy smell. A smell Sam always liked. One of his favourites. Reminded him of spring. Reminded him of walks in the Lake District with Rebecca. Reminded him of ice creams by the beach in Grange-over-Sands, watching the lightning flash in the distance.

Only right now, the smell was mixed with the smell of burning. Of rot. Of death.

And it was mixed with the crushing realisation that there was nothing and nobody here for them to find.

He stood there. Stared at the bodies. So many of them stacked up on each other. They were burned black. Burned to a crisp. And they'd been burned so badly that Sam couldn't identify them if he wanted to.

And as he stood there, watching the flies buzz around them, watching the crows land on them and pluck at them with their long, bloodied beaks, and watching seagulls swoop down too and fight the crows for them, there was only one thing he could think about. And that was Tara.

He looked at those bodies. He had no idea how long they'd been here. But it didn't look or smell like they'd been burned all that long ago. So many questions spiralled around his mind. Was this the NRS? Or had the NRS done this? Were the NRS even still a thing anymore? Where did that leave Rebecca, Leonard, and the others?

And Tara.

Tara and Kurt.

If they were heading north... had they already made it here by the time this attack had occurred?

Had they been caught up in it too?

"Sam," Seann said.

A knot in Sam's stomach. 'Cause he didn't want to speak to Seann. He didn't want to hear Seann's irritating voice of reason like now. 'Cause he knew what Seann was going to say. He knew he was going to be *logical*. He knew he was going to be realistic. He knew what he was going to say to him. Exactly what he was going to say to him. Because Seann was always the fucking same, wasn't he? He'd tell him to quit. He'd tell him to give up. He'd tell him he needed to move on because they needed to move on, because blah blah fucking blah.

But Sam wasn't quitting. He wasn't giving up. He wasn't moving on. Because he couldn't.

"We keep searching," Sam said. Taking a deep breath and standing tall.

Seann sighed. "Sam."

"Stop saying 'Sam'. Just—just fucking say it. If you've got summat to say, then just fucking say it. Or don't. That'd be better."

"Don't do this now."

"I'm not doing *anything*," Sam said, turning around, squaring up to Seann. "I'm not standing around. I'm not moping. I'm—I'm searching this place. I'm searching it, and I'm going to find a trace of the NRS. I'm going to find a trace of her. And then... and then I'll do whatever I have to do."

He turned back around. Walked down the road. There were so many buildings here. So many buildings to be searched. He'd comb every fucking inch of them if he had to. Anything he fucking could if it meant finding a trace of the NRS, if it meant finding a trace of Tara.

"She's gone," Seann said.

Sam stopped. Stopped right there on the spot. And then he turned around to face Seann. "What did you just say?"

Seann shook his head. "I'm sorry, Sam. But it's—you know it was a possibility."

Sam walked back towards Seann. "What did you just say, just then?"

"I said she's gone," Seann said, a little firmer. "And—and I'm sorry. I'm sorry, but it's always been a possibility. But she's gone. She's gone, and there's nothing you can do about it. There's nothing either of us can do about it. But we need to get away from here. We need to start thinking about ourselves. Before... before you get us both killed."

Sam stood right in front of him. Just inches away from him now. His chest was tight. His heart was pounding. And he couldn't think logically. Couldn't think straight.

All he could see was a man standing right before him, telling him everything he'd been working so hard towards had been in vain.

So without thinking, in this foggy state, Sam lifted his rifle.

Pointed it at Seann.

"Get fucked," Sam said.

Seann's eyes widened. "Sam?"

"Don't fucking 'Sam' me anymore," Sam said. Stepping towards Seann. "Don't fucking *anything* me anymore."

"Lower your rifle," Seann said, his voice a little shaky. He was holding a rifle, too. But he wasn't pointing his at Sam.

"Go," Sam said. "I don't want you around anymore. I don't—I don't want any fucking thing to do with you anymore. Just—just go. Fucking go. Or I'll... Don't think I won't shoot you. Don't think I won't fucking shoot you right now."

Seann's face dropped. He looked genuinely mortified. And even though he was still holding his rifle, he was shaking his head. And refusing to lift his rifle. "You wouldn't," he said. "Not after everything we've been through. Not after how far we've—"

"Go!" Sam shouted.

Seann stood there. A few tears building in his bloodshot eyes. He opened his mouth like he was going to speak again. And then he closed it, clearly thinking fucking better of it.

He looked at Sam. Shook his head. And he turned around slowly. And that made Sam feel bad. It made him feel even more guilty. It made him feel even more alone.

But he knew that was how it had to be.

He knew that any sort of connection only led to tragedy.

So he stood there. Even though he wanted to tell Seann to stop, and even though he wanted to apologise to him, he watched him turn around. He watched his head lower. And he watched him start to walk away.

And then Seann stopped.

He looked back.

Looked right into Sam's eyes.

"I thought you were better than this," Seann said. "But—but you've become everything you hated."

And then he turned around, and he walked.

Sam's heart thudded. His nausea intensified. He wanted to tell Seann to stop. To come back here. He wanted to apologise to him and tell him he was just hurting and that he didn't want to be alone.

But all Sam could do was stand there. Pointing his rifle at Seann.

All he could do was watch as he walked further and further away.

And all he could do was wait as Seann grew further into the distance.

And then he was gone.

CHAPTER FORTY-ONE

Sam walked through the streets in search of any trace of Tara and the NRS, but he was beginning to lose hope completely.

It was afternoon. Rainy. Pissing it down. He was drenched. Completely soaked to the skin. He felt cold. Shivery. Shaky. And he just wanted warmth. He just wanted the luxury of warmth all over again. Even though it sounded mopey, and even though he knew he needed to get his act together for thinking that way, he couldn't help it. He just couldn't help it.

He wanted warmth.

He wanted some kind of fucking comfort.

He wanted... Tara.

He looked at these streets. These empty streets. He looked at the abandoned cars. And he looked at all the houses, all the flats, all the old shops. There were so many of them. He'd searched so many of them already, here in this supposed NRS base. And he'd searched them from bottom to top and top to bottom again. But the more he searched, the more it became abundantly clear. The more the horrible inevitability became abundantly clear.

He wasn't going to find Tara here.

He wasn't going to find any trace of the NRS here.

They were gone. Both of them were gone. All of them were gone. And now he was alone.

But... but no. As he walked, he couldn't accept they were gone. As he walked, rifle in hand, he couldn't just accept that Tara had disappeared. He just couldn't. Because she was out there. While there was a chance she was out there, he couldn't give up on her. He had to accept that she wasn't here. He'd walked all this way, and Seann had walked all this way, and they hadn't found her. Neither of them had found her.

But... but that didn't mean she was dead. It didn't mean she was gone. It just meant... Fuck, he didn't know what it meant. Not anymore.

He just wanted to find her. To find a trace of her.

He just wanted to know where she was.

He just wanted... he just wanted that connection all over again.

But the more he walked, that inevitability grew even stronger. That realisation. That acceptance. That acceptance that Tara wasn't here and the chances of finding her *anywhere* were slim to none. He knew that. Deep down, he'd always known it. He'd just been hiding it. Trying to hide from it. Trying to run away from it.

But he couldn't run away from the reality any longer. He couldn't run away from the truth any longer. And the truth was right here, staring him right in the eyes.

He thought of Rebecca. He thought of Leonard. He thought of Harvey, Marky, and Claude. He thought about the moment he'd given up on them in search of Tara. The moment he'd trusted them together. How he'd given up on everything in pursuit of saving Tara and finding Kurt and making that fucker pay for what he'd done.

And then he thought of Seann.

A knot in his chest when he thought of Seann. Real fucking tight. Because... because Seann wasn't a bad person. He wasn't a bad man at all. Not by any stretch of the imagination. And he'd treated him like shit. Pointing that rifle at him. Telling him to walk. Ordering him to walk away or he'd shoot him. That... that was fucking awful. That was fucking unforgivable. Especially after Seann had given everything up for him. Given everything up to help him.

And now he'd pushed Seann away. He'd pushed Seann away, and he was on his own. Completely on his own.

And that was on him.

He looked back over his shoulder. Back to where Seann had disappeared. Part of him wanted Seann to just appear. To just appear out of nowhere again, to walk back here, to tell him they could move on from this and that everything was going to be okay.

But Sam wasn't kidding himself. Sam wasn't a fucking fool. Sam knew that wasn't happening. He'd burned that bridge. He'd burned that bridge, and Seann wasn't coming back for him. He'd done everything Seann had warned him he was going to do; he'd become everything Seann had feared he was going to become.

So this was who he was.

And this was what he had to do.

He took a deep breath. Tears stinging his eyes. He looked around at the community. The buildings. The cars. Everything.

He looked around, took a shaky deep breath.

And as much as he felt lost, and as much as he felt lonely, and as much as he knew the chances of finding Tara or *anyone* right now were slim to none... Sam did the only thing he had left to do. The only option he had left to himself.

Sam kept on searching.

CHAPTER FORTY-TWO

Seann walked away from the town and couldn't shake the hurt and anger he felt—and also the crippling sense of defeat.

But mostly, he just felt sad. Sad for Sam. Sad that this was where their journey had ended up. Sad that this was the result of what they'd experienced together. He was sad that for all their travelling, for as long as they'd been travelling, this was where it ended. With Sam. Sam, pointing a rifle at him and telling him to fuck off.

And the worst thing? Well, not the worst thing—the worst thing was finding a pile of bodies and not finding any trace of this so-called NRS, and not finding any trace of Tara, which Seann always feared would be the case anyway. But the worst thing aside from those?

He still felt sorry for Sam. Because he knew Sam didn't want to shoot him. He knew Sam didn't want to hurt him. He was just in pain. He was in serious pain. He wanted nothing more than to stay there. To support him. 'Cause that bloke was going through a tragedy. Of course, he fucking was. He was bound to be.

But he'd heard the words Sam said to him. And he knew that

he'd put other people before him for far too long. And as much as it scared him, as much as it terrified him... he needed to stop that. Now.

It was time to put himself first.

He looked back over his shoulder. Back down at the remains of the community. The memory of those burned bodies lying there in a pile. He pictured Sam searching through them. Searching through every one of them until he found a trace of Tara. Or didn't find a trace of Tara. And maybe if he *did* find a trace of Tara, he'd just fool himself anyway, tell himself that it might not be her, that it might just be someone *like* her, and there was a chance she was still out there.

Because that's what it was feeling like now. It was feeling like even if Sam found Tara's body right in front of him, he still wouldn't stop searching for her. He still wouldn't give up on her.

And that was dangerous.

It was very fucking dangerous.

He looked back at the community, and he wanted to go back there. He wanted to pull Sam out of that rut he was in. He wanted to tell him to get up and that they had to get away from here. That they had to start living. That they couldn't keep chasing scraps after all anymore.

But on the other hand... he knew it didn't matter what he said to Sam. Sam had been clear with him. Perfectly fucking clear with him. He didn't want him around. He didn't want him near at all.

He wanted him gone.

He took another deep, shaky breath of that cool air. He couldn't pretend he and Sam had the best friendship. But he'd seen something in him. Even when he was being a prick with him, which was admittedly most of the time... he'd seen something underneath that. A good man. A man who he didn't want to see fall into a black hole. A black hole that Seann had been in before and a black hole he didn't want to see anyone else in.

But then he shook his head. Closed his burning eyes. And he remembered something he'd once said.

Life's out of your control. You can only try your best.

And that's exactly what he'd done.

He turned around. Away from the community. And he faced the road ahead. Looked at the sun shining down from above. Looked at the clouds above. And even though he didn't know what awaited him on this road... he knew what he had to do.

He'd tried his best for Sam.

He'd tried his best for Tara.

But now... now, it was time to start trying his best for himself.

He took another deep breath, swallowed a lump in his throat, and then he walked.

IN THE DISTANCE, Carlton watched one of the men who'd murdered his friends in the area, and a smile stretched across his face.

"Looks like we're in luck, folks," he said.

CHAPTER FORTY-THREE

Sam wasn't sure how many times he paced through the community when he finally began to accept he wasn't going to find anything.

He sat back. Sat back against the wall of one of the buildings. He didn't know what the building was. He didn't know what *any* of the buildings were. He didn't know how long he'd been searching this place. But it was still daylight, so it can't have been that long unless he'd lost a frigging day to the search haze, which honestly wouldn't surprise him at this point. It was pissing it down. He was drenched. Soaked to the skin. Shivering. Cold. Hell, he'd been on the go for so many weeks now, and so focused on finding a trace of Tara that he'd kind of not spent the time to realise just how broken he was. Just how exhausted he was. And now, now he was spending the first damned moment actually just sitting here, just taking it all in... it felt like it was all catching up with him.

He sat there, and he started to see the truth in front of him. The bitter reality. Tara wasn't here. Or if she had been here, she wasn't here anymore. Unless she was in that pile of bodies. Sure, it wasn't something he wanted to think about. It wasn't something he wanted to consider, not really. But it was a possibility. And he'd spent far too long fighting logic to see the truth right in front of him all along.

He thought about Seann. Looked up. Outside the walls of this abandoned town. He wondered where he was right now. And as much as he felt a cunt for how he'd dealt with him... he wondered if there might still be a chance there. Because he saw how Seann had stood by him. He saw how much wisdom Seann had spoken to him and how much strength Seann had given him. Because, sure, on the outside, he acted like Seann pissed him off. And he *did* piss him off, sometimes.

But... but that wasn't the deep truth.

The deep truth was that Seann was loyal. And he was wise. And he'd stood by him. He'd helped him. And when others would've walked away, Seann had stayed there.

He thought back to what Seann told him once. About life being out of your control sometimes. How you could only do your best at all times. And he saw it. He saw that was the truth. And he saw something else, too. Something Seann told him. About how not to push others away at the expense of yourself. How focusing on saving Tara so much was going to end up either getting him killed or leaving him alone.

And he saw it. He saw it now. And as painful as it was... he saw it was true. He saw *everything* Seann said was true. And while he was never going to give up on Tara... right now, he knew what he needed. He needed to find Seann. He needed to apologise to him. And whether he accepted it or not... Sam just needed Seann to know that he appreciated everything he'd done for him.

He got up. Walked out of town. Past that mound of bodies, the flies still buzzed around. Absolutely reeked of death. He didn't want to look at it again. Didn't even want to accept what he was looking at. He didn't know who these people were. He didn't know whether they were this NRS or whether they were killed by the NRS. He didn't know a thing.

But as he walked, he knew one thing.

The man he'd met. The man in the cabin. Dave. He thought back to him, and as much as he liked that man—which was a rare thing for Sam at first impression—he also saw him, and he scared him.

Because that was a vision of what Sam was going to become if he didn't attempt to make amends with Seann right now.

And he wasn't doing it out of selfishness. He wasn't doing it out of fear of being alone.

He was doing it because he felt genuinely grateful to Seann. And he was so, so sorry for flipping on him in a moment of tragedy. In a moment of what felt like pure loss.

He walked out of the gates, up the hill, and then he started running. Not once looking back at that community. Because suddenly, his focus had shifted. His focus had shifted to Seann. His focus had shifted to finding him. Finding him before he got too far away. If there was any chance of finding him at all.

But there was this feeling in his chest. This feeling at the pit of his stomach.

A nagging feeling that something was wrong.

He kept on running. Kept on moving up the hill. Exhausted. Panting. Broken. But he had to keep going. He couldn't just give up. He had to keep going, and he had to find him. He had to keep going, and he had to make it.

He kept on going as his hope began to recede. Because— because it'd been ages, hadn't it? He'd been searching the town for ages. So Seann was probably long gone. He'd probably lost him too. He'd probably lost him too, and now he was alone, and he was fucked and...

And then he saw it.

It took him a few seconds to truly recognise what he was looking at. To truly comprehend it. To truly take it in.

But when he saw what it was, when he realised, when it clicked, a knot tightened in his stomach.

His throat went dry.

And his body went numb.

Because in the distance, he could see Seann.

Only Seann wasn't alone.

Two men. Two men running up to him. Attacking him. Swinging fists at him. Punching him. Booting him.

Seann was under attack.

He was in big danger.

And he needed help.

Immediately.

CHAPTER FORTY-FOUR

Kurt stood there in the middle of the town that he was pretty sure was once some kind of sanctuary, and he couldn't believe what he was looking at.

First, the bodies. That pile of bodies lying there in the middle of the road. They were all blackened. All burned. All charred. And he could see from the looks on their faces that they'd been through hell. Probably happened to them while they were alive. Which was awful. Absolutely awful. Kurt had never done that to anyone. Well, okay. Maybe he'd done it to a *few* people. Made the meat taste better, after all. Fresher, somehow. Richer. He'd got that idea from Korea or somewhere like that. Heard they tied up dogs and beat them before killing them for their meat. It was sad, wasn't it? Really sad. Those poor, suffering things.

But at least they could bring joy to others. At least in their sacrifice, they could provide happiness to other people. It was a selfless act in a way, was suffering. Very generous. Very thoughtful.

It was just a shame that the people he'd made suffer weren't exactly so down with the idea themselves.

He looked at those bodies, and he wondered what'd happened here. Something not good, anyway. It looked like someone had burst through this place and massacred the lot of them. Why? A rival group? A viral outbreak? Or no reason whatsoever? Kurt didn't know. And he figured he'd never find out. He never *had* to find out. Not really.

All that mattered was that this was the place he had been searching for. This was the place he was trying to track down for so, so long. This was the place those NRS signs were pointing him towards all along.

And now he was here... it wasn't what he was looking for. It wasn't what he was looking for at all.

It was everything he was trying not to look for.

Everything he was trying not to find.

He stood there in the silence of this abandoned safe haven, and he didn't know what to say. He didn't know what to think. He wasn't expecting to feel this way. After all, he was still alive. And Tara was still here, still by his side. So why was he so down?

And at the end of the day... what had he been expecting to find, really? What had he been hoping for? Sure, he told himself that maybe he was seeking out another chance. He was searching for a new beginning. He was trying to find a new opportunity to start again and forget the past. Because he'd been a leader. And he'd done some horrible, awful things. But maybe... maybe he could start again. Maybe he could be better. Maybe he didn't need to worry anymore.

Maybe he could be the man his parents and his family always wanted him to be.

Not the monster he'd turned into.

But standing here now... Kurt wasn't an emotional man, but he felt an unfamiliar emotion. And that emotion was sadness. It wasn't something he felt very often. He was good at extinguishing his emotions the second they sparked up and threatened to desta-bilise him.

But right now... right now, there was nothing he could do about this emotion. He felt sad. Like a normal person. Because this wasn't the place he was hoping to find. This wasn't the new beginning he was hoping for. This was... this was different entirely.

"What now?"

Tara's voice. A voice he wasn't sure he wanted to hear right now. A voice he wasn't sure how to feel about anymore. Because... because this was the end of the road as far as their journey was concerned. What came after the NRS? Kurt had no idea. I mean, he knew of other people. Other groups he'd done deals with. Other communities in the vicinity. But they all knew who he was. They all knew his reputation. And the second they knew what'd happened to *his* community, they weren't going to just let him live after the hell he'd put them through.

So this really was a new beginning for Kurt. This really was an attempt to start again—properly. And maybe one day, when he felt strong enough again, maybe he *would* rise up. Maybe he *would* try to recreate what he'd started at the industrial estate and rule over a new set of people—convert a new group to his ways.

But right now... right now, he was content with just surviving. He was content with just company. And that was something Tara had taught him.

He looked at her. So pale. So thin. So exhausted. But so beautiful. And he realised he felt something. He realised, deep inside, he felt something. Something he hadn't felt about anyone else for a long, long time. Something he'd been trying to push away. Something he'd been trying to resist feeling; trying to resist comprehending. But something he couldn't deny. The reason he'd kept her around. The real reason, underneath all the bullshit.

And that reason was he felt something about her.

He actually *felt* something.

And that was terrifying.

"We made it," Tara said. "Congratu-fucking-lations. And now we're here... it's not what you were looking for. It's not what we wanted to find at all. So what now?"

And as Kurt looked at Tara, listening to her vocalise his own thoughts, he realised that this bond he had with her was becoming dangerous. This sense of connection he was beginning to feel with her... it was problematic. And it was something he had to avoid. Something he had to suppress.

But it wasn't something he felt like he could suppress much longer.

He went to open his mouth and speak—what he was planning to say, he had no idea—and then he saw something.

Off in the distance. Walking towards this town. Not just one. But two. Two men.

Two men that, as they got closer, he realised he recognised.

"What're you gawping at?" Tara asked, turning around. "What's..."

And then she stopped, too. She stopped speaking right there. Of course, she did. Because she'd seen these men. She'd seen them too.

And just like Kurt, she realised who they were, too.

"Well, well," Kurt said, a smile widening across his face and cutting through all his prior sense of disappointment. "What do we have here?"

He looked up the hill towards the two men approaching.

He looked at the one who called himself Sam.

And he smiled.

Shit was about to get very, very interesting.

CHAPTER FORTY-FIVE

Sam saw Seann in the distance, and he knew he couldn't just leave him there.

Because if he left him there, he was going to die.

He could see him on the ground. He could see these men booting him. Burying their boots into his chest. Into his neck. Into his face. It didn't look like they'd gone any harder than that. At least not yet. But Sam knew what people were like. He knew it couldn't be long. So he needed to do something about it before that happened.

He ran. Ran up the slope, over towards those men, raising his rifle in the process. If he could get a clean shot at them from here, he might be okay. He might be able to actually help Seann from a distance. But it was risky. Shooting from this far was risky. Way too risky. And it was a risk he wasn't sure he was willing to take. Not again.

He ran up the slope, rifle raised. Part of him wanted to be subtle. Another part of him knew he didn't have the *time* to be subtle. He just had to keep on running. He just had to help Seann. He had to help him, no matter what it took.

He kept his focus on the men and Seann as he ran up the hill when suddenly he felt something whoosh past his face.

He didn't realise what it was. Not at first. Not until he heard that bang echoing in his ears, a delayed reaction. And not until he felt a burning right across his cheek.

A bullet.

Someone had shot at him.

Someone had—

Another bang in the distance. Another bullet whizzing towards him. Not from the ones beating Seann up but from someone else. From somewhere else. Someone and somewhere he couldn't see.

He tried to focus on where they were coming from—but focus was hard when his life was on the fucking line. He tried to squint ahead as he ran further and further up that hill, pointing the rifle up ahead. He tried to focus, and he tried to stay here and stay with it. Because if didn't—if something happened to him—then Seann was dead, too. And Sam couldn't have that. Not in an "on his conscience" way, which just reeked of self-pity. But in a literal couldn't have that way. He cared about Seann. He didn't want anything happening to him. He didn't want him dying. And Sam had to do something about that.

He heard another bang and felt another bullet whizz past him when he dropped to the ground.

He lay there. Face flat on the road. Heart racing. Rifle in hand. He squinted into the distance through the light, thin pieces of glass up in front of him. He looked ahead towards the direction that bullet had come from. That direction which someone had shot at him from. He tried to see them as his heart raced. Tried to see them as he shook with the adrenaline. He tried to see them... but he couldn't. He just couldn't see them.

He stayed there. Flat on his belly. Which was such a hard thing to do when he could hear Seann being beaten in the distance.

When he could hear the cracking of his ribs as feet hit them. When he could hear him wincing and yelping. When he could hear him *trying* to fight back but failing. He was dying. He was dying right in front of Sam, and right now, Sam couldn't do a thing about it.

He needed to get up. He needed to keep running. And he needed to take a risk. He needed to fire in their direction, even if it meant he missed them. Even if it ran the risk of hitting Seann. Because if he didn't risk it, Seann was definitely dead. Definitely. And if he risked it... well, there was a chance he'd hit him. But at least there was a chance he could save him, too.

He went to stand up, fully expecting another barrage of bullets to come flying his way when suddenly he saw something.

Right there in the distance, Sam saw movement.

Movement. A figure. A figure walking towards him. Holding a rifle. The rifle he'd taken off Seann by the looks of things. A woman.

He took a deep breath. Swallowed a lump in his throat. They were getting close. Very close. Holding that rifle. And if Sam could just keep his head down, if he could just avoid attracting any attention, then maybe there was a way out of this. Maybe this didn't go the way he thought it might go.

He watched that woman walk closer and closer towards him. Rifle only partly raised now.

Watched her look over in his direction.

And for a moment, as Sam lay there, he thought she'd seen him. He thought she'd made eye contact with him. Thought she'd looked right at him.

He lifted his rifle.

He took another deep breath.

Held it.

And then he pulled the trigger.

It all happened so fast. The way she fell to the ground. The blood that spurted out of her head. And the way the sound of her thudding against the ground cut through the sound of Seann's yelps and the sound of the ringing echoing in Sam's ears.

He lay there, and he saw she was gone, and he knew that now was his moment.

Now was his opportunity.

Now was his chance.

He went to stand and run towards them and save Seann when suddenly he heard something right behind him.

Something that made him freeze.

Something that made the hairs on the back of his neck stand right on end.

As Sam began to run, he heard something that changed everything.

"Sam?"

A voice.

A voice right behind him.

A voice he'd recognise from a mile away.

Tara's voice.

CHAPTER FORTY-SIX

Sam heard Tara's voice, and everything changed.

Suddenly, in an instant, he didn't hear Seann being beaten in the distance. Suddenly, he didn't see him having the shit kicked out of him by those men. He didn't see any of that at all.

All Sam heard was Tara's voice.

He stood there. Frozen. He wasn't sure whether to turn around. Wasn't fully sure if it was in his head or not. Maybe he'd fucked his ears up pulling that trigger. Maybe the bang was a bit too loud. He wasn't sure. Didn't have a clue.

But as he stood there shaking, he started to realise that he hadn't imagined it. He hadn't imagined it at all. It wasn't in his head. He wasn't crazy. He knew what he'd heard. Exactly what he'd heard.

It was Tara.

Somewhere, somehow, it was Tara.

He turned around. Looked over his shoulder. A part of him afraid. A big part of him in denial over whether he was even going to see her there at all.

But as he looked over his shoulder, he saw her in the distance, and he knew he couldn't hide from the truth.

Tara was standing there. Staring at him. She looked pale. She looked thin. She had big circles under her eyes. And she looked exhausted. Truly exhausted.

But she was here. She was alive.

Only she wasn't alone.

There was someone else here with her. Someone Sam recognised very well. Very well, indeed. Someone that made his toes curl. Someone that sparked a hatred deep inside him. That made him remember how angry he was. How vengeful he was. And how much he wanted to see this man suffer.

He was standing behind her. Smiling. Towering over her. He was so tall. And somehow, he looked... he looked even creepier and scarier than Sam remembered. Even more intimidating.

And seeing him here, seeing him standing here with Tara... it made a wave of hatred crash over him as he held his rifle. Because he was so close. He was so close that Sam could take him out in an instant. But at the same time... it was just so risky. Shooting him was putting Tara in danger. In big, big danger. And that was not something he wanted to do.

But Tara. The woman he'd been searching for. The woman he'd started to lose hope of finding at all. She was here. She was right here, and he had to do something. He had to help her. He had to *try*.

He went to walk towards her, towards Kurt, towards the pair of them, when suddenly he heard Seann behind him.

A yelp. A real pained yelp. And hearing it... Hearing it brought him crashing right back into the moment. Hearing it made him snap back into reality like he was in a dream, and suddenly he was waking up. And it made his stomach sink. Because Seann. Tara might be here, and Kurt might be here with her. But Seann was in trouble. He was in serious trouble. And Sam couldn't just leave him. He couldn't just abandon him. He couldn't just leave everyone to die.

But then... Tara.

Tara was everything he cared about. Tara was everything he'd gone on this journey for. Tara was everything to him. And seeing her here now, right in front of him... he could see her standing here, and then he could envision Kurt doing something to her right in front of Sam just to punish them both. He could picture him killing her right before him, just like he'd done with Millie.

He stood there, knot tightening his stomach. Sickliness rising in his throat. He felt dizzy. Sick. Wanted to vomit. Wanted to throw up everywhere. He felt exhausted, emotionally and physically. And he wasn't sure what to do right now. He wasn't sure what to do at all.

He loved Tara. And he was filled with so much regret over how they'd gone their separate ways. And so much love for her. He couldn't actually believe she was here. He couldn't actually believe that after everything, she was right here. He'd found her. He'd found her again. And she was alive.

And this was everything he had been looking for. This was everything he had been searching for. And yet... there was someone else who needed him more right now. Someone who was in danger. Someone who was suffering.

And even though a few days ago—even a few hours ago—he might've acted differently... right now, he saw things differently. He saw things very differently. Because Seann was right. All along, he was right. He was just trying to push other people away because he was too scared to bond. But right now, Seann needed him most. And that's what he had to do. Tara wasn't everything to him. He loved her. And he was going to fight for her. But right now... there was someone who needed him more.

"You can't save everyone," Kurt said. Chuckling.

And Sam felt a knot tighten in his chest as he looked into

Tara's eyes. "I know," he said. "But I... I also have faith in you. To save yourself."

He saw Tara's eyes lighten up. Saw them widen. Saw her nod at him as he nodded back at her.

And then, as much as it went against every single instinct in his body, Sam turned around.

He looked back over at Seann, who was still having the shit kicked out of him.

He lifted his rifle.

It was time to save Seann.

It was time to make his choice.

CHAPTER FORTY-SEVEN

Seann lay on the ground and felt the boot smack against his face again, and he literally had no idea how long he had left.

He could taste blood. He could feel loose teeth, all jagged in his mouth, nicking against his tongue. His face was on fire. And his ears were ringing like an explosion had gone off nearby. Maybe it had. He wasn't sure. Didn't know at all. Just that he was in pain. He was in pain, and he was in agony, and he wasn't sure how he was ever going to get out of this mess.

He lay there on the ground, and he felt these men beating him over and over. Squinted up at them. He tried to get back to his feet. Tried to stand. But every time he mustered up an ounce of strength to get back up, another boot would slam against his face. Or another fist would crack into his chest. He felt broken. He felt weak. He felt like even if by some miracle he got out of this mess, he'd still be in deep shit. Because he'd been beaten to within an inch of his life. And that inch was rapidly disappearing by the second.

So as much as he tried to hold on, as much as he did what he felt was natural to him, he found himself closing his eyes. He found himself managing the crippling pain in his body the only way he could. He was in a wood somewhere. A nice, luscious wood. The smell of fresh leaves in the air. The sound of birds singing all around. And the warmth of the sun contrasting the coolness from the shade of the trees, all enveloping him in this bliss. Somewhere in the distance, he could hear seagulls. And he could hear waves. The waves of the ocean. He could smell the sea salt. He could taste it in the air, too. Not blood. Not teeth. Not the imminent clutches of death that felt like they were getting closer. He could taste... happiness.

He lay there in these woods, and he listened to the birds, and he felt the warmth of the sun and the coolness of the breeze, and he felt for some reason like he wasn't alone. He could still feel the pain of his beating. He was still aware of that. But it was kind of like when you were uncomfortable when you were asleep or had a telly on in the background or something. You might be aware of it, but it wasn't enough to get in the way. Not anymore.

He turned around, and he saw Colin standing there.

Colin looked as gorgeous as he'd always looked. Tall. Well-tanned. Handsome. And just seeing him made Seann simultaneously happy and sad. Happy because he looked so lifelike, so real, far more crystal clear than any product of his imagination recently. But it was also sad, too. Because as much as he wanted to believe that this was Colin, and that he was real, and that he was still here... he knew deep down that wasn't the case. Colin was gone. He was long gone.

He sat right down beside Seann. Didn't say anything. Didn't speak at first. He didn't have to. His presence alone was enough.

And then Seann heard him. "Nice spot."

Seann looked at him. Smiled. "Thanks. I created it myself."

Colin raised an eyebrow. "You always were the creative one."

"We both know that's not true," Seann said.

He sat there looking into Colin's eyes. And he felt himself

tearing up a little. "Look at us," he said. "You're missing, and I'm about to die. It's not ideal, is it?"

"No. It's not ideal."

And then Colin reached over for him. Went to touch his hand. And it was that touch that Seann had missed so much. It was that touch that made him feel like life was worth living. That reminded him he was loved after a bad day. It was that touch that he would never, ever forget, no matter how much his memories might fade.

He felt Colin's hand get closer to him. And then, out of nowhere, when it was so close, Colin pulled it away.

"What's up?" Seann asked.

And Colin looked right at him. Smiling now.

"What?" Seann said. "What—what is it?"

Colin took a deep breath. The sun shining right behind him, making him harder to see now. "I don't think you're ready."

"Ready for what?"

Colin's smile widened even more. "I think you know what."

He saw Colin close his eyes and lean in to kiss him as that light filled his eyes when suddenly, out of nowhere, he heard something.

A bang.

A bang.

He opened his eyes.

He was on the ground. On the ground in the cloud and the rain. He was cold. He was in agony. His body ached all over, and his mouth was filled with the taste of blood. His eyes felt all swollen. His head was banging. He couldn't think straight.

But he'd heard a bang.

He looked up through his blurred vision, and he saw someone standing there, right ahead of him.

A man. A man standing over him. One of the ones who had been beating him up.

Only...

His eyes were wide. His face was pale. And he was choking. Clutching his bleeding throat and choking.

He fell to one side, and Seann saw someone else standing there.

He couldn't make him out. Not properly. Not in the blurriness of his vision. But he was standing there, holding a rifle. Pointing it by Seann's side at one of the other men.

"No," the other man said, with his whiny voice. "Please," he said. "Don't—don't do this. Don't—"

Another bang.

The man's head exploded right beside him. Fragments of skull breaking off and landing on the ground beside Seann.

And as Seann lay there, as he lay on his back, the warmth of the blood from these two men splattering against him, he smiled.

He smiled because of who was above him.

He smiled, and he cried because of who was here for him.

When he saw him come into view properly, he smiled even more.

Sam held out a hand. Went to lift Seann to his feet. "Come on," he said. "Let's get you out of here."

And when Sam's hand touched his, he saw Colin in his mind's eye, and he didn't feel the pain anymore.

CHAPTER FORTY-EIGHT

Kurt stood there and stared up the road and couldn't believe quite what he'd just witnessed.

Sam. Sam, standing there. Staring down the hill towards him. Holding a rifle. See, Kurt had been here a little while. He'd watched Sam enter the town. He'd seen the reaction on his face as he searched it, with Seann by his side, trying to reassure him all the time—and trying to convince him that they had to leave. And all the while, he'd watched. He'd watched, and Tara had watched alongside him, and even though it hurt a little that Tara made it so damned clear that she'd rather be with Sam than with him... still, he couldn't help the smirk across his face. Because he saw what was going to happen. He saw exactly what had to happen.

He was going to kill Tara right in front of Sam.

That spark of his old life. That memory of the power-crazy man he used to be. It all came sneaking back inside him. His desire for a new life, for a more honourable life—for, God forbid, a life where *Tara* meant something to him—that was gone now. And in its place, he saw a man who he believed was responsible for the downfall of his community. He'd let him go. And Sam hadn't played ball. He'd got away. And then the rest of his people had got away—most of them, anyway. And now here he was. Here he was, staring down the slope at the woman he clearly fucking loved, and Kurt suddenly felt that streak of old returning. That desire of old returning.

That desire for power. That desire to cause pain.

And that realisation that it didn't matter how much he tried to trick himself... he just wasn't like everyone else. He was different. And instead of running away from that, instead of trying to bury it and convince himself otherwise, he needed to embrace it.

His old mum used to always bang on at him to be himself. To be proud of who he was. Well, Mum, it's time to take you at your motherfucking word.

But... but something else happened. Something he didn't expect. Sam. He didn't come running down towards him like Kurt expected. He didn't come launching at him in a moment of vengeance as Kurt expected. Instead... instead he did something completely against Kurt's expectations.

He looked at Tara. Said something to her. Said something to her about trusting her. About how she could do this.

And then he turned around, and he ran in the other direction.

And Kurt found himself standing there. Frozen. Somewhat panicked. Because—because he wasn't used to not being in control. Even when he was at a loss, there was still a part of him that was in control.

But this... for some reason, this threw him. This threw him more than anything.

He looked around at Tara. And he saw the way she was looking at him. Almost like... almost like she felt sorry for him. Not sorry for herself. But sorry for him. Like she was looking at him with pity, somehow.

And Kurt didn't feel comfortable with that. He didn't like how it made him feel, that she looked sad. Because... because he found he didn't *want* her to be sad. He didn't want her to be sad at all.

He wanted her to be happy. Because as much as it pained his poisoned heart to admit it, he felt something for her. A weakness for her. And he felt bad that she felt abandoned.

And that was... conflicting.

Because he wanted to crush her. He wanted to crush her and the way she made him feel. Because that was problematic. And that was wrong. And that was something he couldn't allow. Not anymore.

But on the other hand...

On the other hand, there was another voice in his head. A voice telling him that maybe there was still something there for him. Maybe there was still a chance.

A chance of a normal life.

He looked into Tara's sad eyes. He reached out. Touched her face. Stroked her hair from her forehead. "Don't—don't worry," he said. "I've got you."

And Tara moved towards him slowly. Like she was getting ready to bury her head in his chest. Like she was getting ready to feel that warmth of his. And he felt like a kid all over again. He felt like he'd felt when Julia Breaker had shown an interest in him. He felt his guard dropping just like it had when he was younger. Only this was... this was different. This didn't feel as dangerous. And it never dawned on him that this might be even *more* danger-ous, such was the power of love...

He felt like she was moving towards him and like she had seen who he really was but still saw something in him.

He felt that warmth inside his body that powered over all reason and felt her wrap her arms around him.

"It's okay," Kurt said. Holding her. "Don't—don't be sad."

"I'm not sad," Tara said. "Not for me."

Kurt felt his eyes narrow. "What—"

"Keeping your syringes in your left pocket isn't always the best idea."

And then he felt something.

A sharp scratch. Right in his neck.

A sickening realisation as he stepped back, his eyes widening.

As he saw that syringe of muscle relaxant—the last damned lot he had left—in her shaking hand.

And as he touched his stinging neck and saw that speck of blood.

Tara stood there. Wide-eyed. Staring at him. "You—you bitch," Kurt said. "You—you evil.... You evil..."

"I could've killed you right here," Tara said. "Like I promised I would."

Kurt tried to stagger towards her as his muscles weakened. He tried to clamber towards her as his limbs grew heavier and heavier. He tried to muster up the strength, just a little more strength, to wrap his hands around this bitch's throat and put her down, once and for all.

"But I think a quick, easy death is too good for you," she said.

He reached out a shaking, weak hand.

He tried to reach out. Tried to grab her. As his heart raced, and as sweat poured down his face.

And then he fell to his knees.

When he fell to his knees, in this cloud of weakness, he felt sadness. He felt betrayal. Because he'd been vulnerable. He'd allowed himself to be vulnerable. And it had caught him. In the end, it had got the better of him.

He sat there and saw Tara staring down at him. Syringe in hand. Smiling.

And behind her, right behind her, as his vision grew more and more blurry, he saw those two people approaching.

Those two *men* approaching down the hill.

"Rest up, Kurt," Tara said. "You've got a long old day ahead of you."

He tried to open his mouth, tried to speak, tried to say anything at all.

But saliva just frothed at his lips.

Trickled down his chin.

And as he battled and tried to convince himself he was strong enough, that he could keep his eyes open, that he was stronger than these drugs because he wasn't human, he wasn't like the rest of them, he was Kurt, and he was a fucking machine... he realised he was kidding himself.

He opened his mouth. And only one word came out. Just the one. "I'll..."

And then he fell face flat onto the road, and darkness surrounded him.

All he heard were those footsteps inching closer.

All he saw in his mind's eye was Tara, standing over him, so damned gorgeous, a smile across her face.

And all he saw ahead of him was the inevitable pain that was to follow...

CHAPTER FORTY-NINE

Sam saw Tara standing right there in front of him, and he still couldn't quite believe what he was looking at.

She looked exhausted. She looked pale. Tired. Dark circles under her eyes. She had sores all over her bare knees, and her forearms looked scratched and bruised. She looked like she'd been through the wringer. Like she'd been through some kind of hell. Which she had. She'd been here with Kurt. God knows what that bastard had done to her.

But she was here. She was alive. This wasn't a dream.

He stood there. Shaking. Unable to speak. Unable to notice any of the rest of his surroundings. All he could see was Tara. All he could see was her standing there, right before him. Shaking too. Syringe in hand. And there was a look of distrust in her eyes. There was a look of uncertainty. Like she didn't trust Sam. Like there was a fragment of a memory of him still there in her mind, but she didn't fully trust him yet.

And he felt so sorry about that. Because the last time he'd seen her properly, they'd been torn apart from each other in the cruellest of circumstances. Reunited and then torn apart by Kurt's thugs.

And the time before that... they'd had their fallout. They'd had their disagreement. They'd gone their separate ways, which Sam knew was the worst damned thing that had ever happened to him. The worst decision of his entire fucking life. He regretted it. He regretted it so much.

But she was here now.

She was here.

He'd found her.

And...

He looked to his left. Saw Seann sitting there. He wasn't in a great way. He was bleeding. He'd been battered. And he was bruised. But... but he was alive too. He wasn't dead. Sam had saved him.

And as Sam looked at him, then looked at Tara, he felt like this was what everything had been building towards. He felt like this was the culmination of his entire journey—his entire *personal* journey.

Everything had been building to this. And now he'd found her. He'd found her, and he was still alive. He'd found her, and Seann was still alive.

And Kurt was lying on the ground right in front of her.

He looked at Kurt. Felt that anger seeping through his veins. Felt that hatred stirring in his body. He detested him. Detested him for what he'd done. Detested him for the things he'd put the people Sam cared about through. Because he didn't care what happened to himself. He could *take* whatever happened to himself. But other people... the people closest to him... that was a different story altogether.

He looked up at Tara. Saw the way she stared over at him. And he couldn't resist or hold back any longer.

He rushed over towards her, and she rushed right over towards him.

He felt her. Felt her fall into his arms. He felt her warmth right there against his chest. And suddenly, everything else disappeared into the background, into irrelevance. The rain. The cloudy skies. All of it disappeared. Suddenly none of it mattered. None of it mattered at all. Only Tara. Only Tara, right here, right now.

He felt her hands against his back, and he kissed her head. And she kissed his cheek. And he wanted to kiss her properly. He wanted to kiss her on the lips, but instead, he just felt that warmth sinking further into his chest; felt her body getting closer and closer, bridging a gap that had been formed between them for so, so long.

"I missed you," Sam said.

And Tara tucked herself in deeper. Hearing his vulnerability—his rare vulnerability. "I missed—I missed you too."

They held each other tight for what felt like forever, and yet like no time at all. And then eventually, after this time bubble passed, he pulled himself a way a little. Looked right into her tearful eyes.

"I always had faith," Sam said.

"What?"

"I always—I always had faith. In you. And that—and that you were strong enough. To save yourself. And that's... and that's because..."

He looked around, then. Saw Seann sitting there. Battered. Bloodied. Bruised. But alive. Alive and upright.

"Don't mind me," Seann said, scratching his head. "It'll be a little sore in the morning. But I'll get by."

He smiled at Seann. Tara smiled at Seann. They all smiled at each other. And as they stood there, together in this town, reunited, Sam wanted this moment to last forever. He wanted this moment standing by the pile of dead, burned bodies to last forever. He never wanted this feeling to end.

And then he looked down at Kurt's unconscious body, and he felt another emotion. A sense of urgency. Deep in his gut.

"What're we going to do about him?" Sam asked.

Tara took an audible deep breath. Cleared her throat. "I think I know exactly what we're going to do about him."

CHAPTER FIFTY

When Kurt opened his eyes, he saw something that terrified him.

Darkness. Total darkness.

He tried to move his wrists, but he couldn't. They were trapped. Tightly bound behind him. He tried to move his ankles, but they were tied, too. He could taste something in his mouth. Something strong and metallic. Blood. And as he sat there, absorbed in the darkness, he felt like he was transporting into the minds and the perspectives of all the people he'd captured. Of all the people he'd held at the warehouse. Of all those prisoners he'd kept, and the misery he'd caused them.

And although he'd been able to distance himself from them, although he'd been able to detach himself from it all... he couldn't deny what he was feeling right now. The emotion he was feeling right at the forefront.

Fear.

He sat there. In the darkness. He tried to move again, tried to break free, but his muscles felt weak and weary. That bitch. Tara. She'd slammed that injection needle into his throat. Pushed that relaxant into his system. He should've known better than to trust her. He should've known better than to let her get anywhere near close.

He felt... betrayed. And that made him feel a little weak to admit, too. He felt betrayed by Tara. Because he'd felt something for her. He'd allowed himself to be vulnerable around her. He'd allowed himself to get somewhat *close* to her. And that was a mistake. That was a serious mistake.

But then... he couldn't exactly blame her for that, could he? He couldn't really blame anyone but himself. It was his decision to be vulnerable. That was his doing. That was his mistake. And he'd got himself in this mess. A mess that, the more he sat here, the more he struggled, and the more his inner sense of fear grew... the more he realised wasn't going to change. He wasn't going to be able to do anything about this.

It was quite fitting in a way, wasn't it? It was rather typical in a sense. Because this was what *he'd* done to people. This was how *he* had treated people. How he'd left them. So it was somewhat... well, poetic, that this was how Sam and Tara had decided to punish him for his crimes. He didn't know where he was. He didn't know what they had planned for him. He had no idea whether they were just going to leave him here, alone, or whether they were going to keep him alive. Feed him. Give him water. Just enough to keep him alive, just like he'd done to them.

And then he heard the shuffling. The footsteps, right in front of him.

He turned. Turned towards that movement. But it was pointless. He couldn't see anything for the darkness. For the blindfold around his head.

He felt another twinge of fear prick up inside him. The uncertainty. The uncertainty of who was in here with him. The uncertainty of what they were going to do about him. The uncertainty of how they were going to treat him or what they were going to do to him at all.

He sat there. Heart racing. Chest tight. Staring into that

darkness. He didn't know what was coming. He didn't know what was next. But whatever was coming, he knew for a fact it wasn't good.

He felt movement right in front of him, and then suddenly, he saw light.

Well. Not light, exactly. It was still dark in this room he was in. Looked like some sort of cabin. Some sort of disused, abandoned cabin. It smelled like shit in here. Unless that was him. He knew he didn't smell all that great, so it was a possibility.

He looked around the cabin, and he saw them standing there, right over him.

Sam. Tara. Both standing there. Both looking down at him.

And he'd never felt afraid of them. He'd never feared them. Not really. Not at all.

But right now... Right now, he felt fear.

Because of what they were holding in their hands.

Tara was holding a screwdriver. Sam was holding a meat cleaver. The rifle that he'd been holding before was at the back of the room. Sitting there, out of reach.

"Look at you," Kurt said, spitting out blood. "Taking the moral high ground. Acting like—like the things I did were inhumane. I told you, we're not so different. We can't be. Because we've made it this far."

Sam stepped forward. He walked right up to Kurt. Stared right into his eyes. "Oh, we have morals," Sam said. "We know what's right. We know what's wrong. We don't make people suffer. Without reason."

"So you're the morality police now?"

Sam punched him across the face. Hard. And then he grabbed the back of his neck. Pressed the meat cleaver to his throat. "I want to murder you for what you've done to us," Sam said. "I want to kill you myself for the things you've done to me. And the people I care about."

Kurt smiled. Even though he was fearful and even though he

was in pain, he smiled. "Then go on. Do it. But you do this, and you know we're not so different."

Sam pushed the meat cleaver so hard against Kurt's neck that he felt like the insides of his throat were about to burst and spill out.

And then he stepped back.

Pulled that cleaver away.

"I'd love to," Sam said. "Like I say. But it's not my decision to make."

Kurt didn't understand. For a moment, another incident of confusion. Another moment of unknowing. Of unpredictability, which always made him fearful. What was he talking about? Why wasn't he...

And then he saw his answer right in front of him.

Tara.

Standing there. Staring down at him. Hatred in her eyes.

Kurt smiled. "Ahh," he said. "I see how it is."

Tara walked over to him. Slowly. Catching that screwdriver in hand. Every step she took felt like forever. Echoing against the walls of this abandoned garage, wherever the hell it was.

She crouched right opposite him. Put a hand on his shoulder. And as she looked into his eyes with those bloodshot eyes of her own, he felt that twinge of betrayal again. A twinge of betrayal and also of shame. Shame for letting his guard drop. Shame for allowing himself to feel. Shame for letting her get so close.

"So this is how it is," Kurt said. "I keep you alive. I spare you. Hell, I even look after you. And this is what it comes to?"

Tara leaned in close. "More fool you."

Kurt shook his head. "And I'm supposed to believe you're just going to drop all your morals right now, Tara? I know you. Don't you forget that. I know... I know you're inherently *good*. And I know that's your weakness. Because if it wasn't your weakness... you would've taken every opportunity you had to kill me while you had the chance."

She looked at him. Stared closely into his eyes. And he couldn't get a read on her. That's what he found difficult. That's what he found... *confusing*. He couldn't get a read on her. And that felt... problematic.

And then she did something else he didn't expect.

She stroked the side of his face with her cold, shaky hand.

"I'm sorry for the life you've lived," Tara said. "And that's... that's the truth. I'm sorry you've suffered so much in your life that you've ended up the way you are. Because I pity you. I don't fear you. I pity you."

She was silent. Silent, for a few seconds.

"But don't mistake my pity for mercy. In no way. Because I made you a promise. Remember?"

Kurt frowned. "What—"

And then it all happened so fast.

She pulled back that screwdriver.

"I made a promise I'd get my revenge. And I'd make you suffer for what you did to Millie. And I'll have no moral fucking objections about that."

And then she buried that screwdriver deep into his left eyeball.

Kurt felt a sudden hot blast of pain. Felt something—*heard* something—burst in his skull. He didn't want to show fear. He didn't want to show agony. He didn't want to show any sign of weakness. Any sign of weakness whatsoever.

But he couldn't help himself.

He screamed.

He screamed, and he begged. Because this was some kind of test. This was some kind of test to break his resolve and put him through pain and make him apologise and beg and—

And then she yanked that screwdriver out of his left eye, in that blinding agony and in that burning haze, and he saw her hovering above him, encircled in a halo of light.

"This is for Millie," she said. Pulling back that screwdriver.

"This is for everyone you put through hell. Everyone you raped. Everyone you killed."

And then she swung the screwdriver right at his right eye.

Held it there, right in front of it, for just a second.

"This is for *me*."

And then she pushed the screwdriver against his eyeball.

She started with gentle pressure at first. And then she started to push harder. And he could feel that pressure building inside his right eye. He could feel the tension growing. He could feel the eyeball shifting shape like it was a balloon filled with water getting ready to burst. He could feel that sharp edge of the screwdriver digging further and further into his eyeball.

And all he could do was scream.

All he could do was scream as he felt blood pooling down his face. All he could do was cry as he felt searing, splitting agony right across his forehead. All he could do was beg as she pushed down harder, harder...

"This is for Millie," she said again, in a haze.

Pushed harder.

"This is for *me*."

And then she pushed with the last bit of strength she had.

An explosion.

A dull ache all across the right side of his face.

And then that screwdriver kept on going.

Kept on going as warm, sticky goo rolled down his cheek—the goo from his eyes as he sat there, blinded by an intense flashing light.

He felt that screwdriver keep on going. Keep on pushing deeper and deeper.

And for a moment, as the pain grew more intense, as he tried to break free, as he screamed for mercy... Kurt felt something he hadn't felt in a long time. Maybe something he hadn't ever felt.

Kurt felt regret.

Not for himself.

But for the things he'd done.

"I'm sorry," he blubbered, as blood and tears and eyeball juice slipped down his face. "For Millie. For—for—"

Another burst of light,.

Another flash of pain.

Another sharp jolt right in the middle of his head.

And then, in that moment of regret, in that moment of agony... Kurt felt nothing.

CHAPTER FIFTY-ONE

Sam stood at the town gates and stared out at the rising sun.

He could hear the birds singing in the sky above. He could feel the cool breeze blowing against his face. There was a warmth to the air still. Like the oncoming autumn and the summer that had passed were in a battle with each other, and neither was winning out at the moment. But there was no resisting the inevitable. There was no changing what was going to happen. Because nature was going to win. Nature *always* won out. That was just how things went, wasn't it? That was a lesson he'd learned. More recently than he perhaps should have. Not that the seasons always changed. None of that bullshit. But more... well. That life was completely out of your control. That sometimes, you just had to accept that life moved in mysterious ways. And there was no way of knowing how it was going to go. But you just had to try your best to adapt to the circumstances.

He heard footsteps. Footsteps, right beside him, approaching him. A twinge of fear when he first heard those footsteps. Which was natural. If you'd been through everything Sam had been through and claimed you didn't feel a slight sense of fear every fucking time you heard some footsteps, you were lying.

But when Sam turned around and saw who was approaching, his fears were alleviated immediately.

He saw Tara. And he saw Seann. Both of them were limping. Both of them looked broken. Both of them were weak. But... but they were here. They were here, and that was all that mattered. They were here. They'd survived. They'd survived the hell they'd been through. They'd survived against all odds. And they were still here.

He looked back over at that old garage in the distance. The one where they'd dealt with Kurt. He thought about how Tara had left him. The things she'd done to him. He thought about the screams he'd let out. The way his eyeless face stared back at him, dripping blood. He thought of all these things. It was haunting, in a way. Because as much as Kurt had deserved everything he'd been put through... it was a side to Tara he hadn't expected to see. A side he didn't know she had in her.

"Early riser," Tara muttered as she approached.

Sam grunted.

"You know how he is," Seann added. "Absolute nightmare. No chance of a lie in when this one is around."

He heard them laughing. Heard them joking. And as much as it was somewhat painful because they were weak and they'd been through hell... it was also nice. Because it reminded him that they still had their humanity. Even after everything they'd been through, everything they'd been put through, they still had their humanity.

They might just be clinging on. But they still had that human-ity. And that was something.

He saw them walk up to him. Saw them standing there. Felt Seann's presence right by his side. He'd taken a risk for Seann. Made the biggest sacrifice of all for Seann. Because that moment when he'd seen Tara, and he'd seen Kurt. Every instinct in his body had screamed at him to go after her. To go after her and help her and make Kurt pay.

But instead... instead, he hadn't.

He'd gone back for Seann. Because Seann was in bigger immediate danger. And he had faith in Tara to look after herself. That was another lesson he'd learned. That he didn't need to save *everyone*. That it was impossible to save everyone.

He could only try his best. And that was life.

"So what now?" Tara asked.

Sam took a deep breath. He didn't know what was next. He didn't know where Rebecca was. He didn't know where Claude was. He didn't know where Leonard was, and where Marky was, and where Harvey was.

But they weren't going to give up finding them. And not because of this saviour complex he'd grappled so desperately with. But because they were here. And they had a chance. And because they had that chance... they were going to try their best. Try their very best.

And that was all they could do.

He looked at Tara. Right into her eyes. And he thought about that moment he'd turned away from her. When he'd turned his back on her, and he'd gone after Seann. He thought about that moment a lot. Why he'd done it. What had happened at that moment. What had shifted. And he realised... he realised it wasn't anything to do with caring or not caring or anything like that. It was quite simple in the end. It was that realisation that his fear of losing people close to him hadn't been driving him—it had been crippling him. It had been holding him back. And that wasn't going to happen again. Not anymore.

He looked at Tara, and he looked at Seann, and then he took a deep breath. "We're going to try our best to find somewhere safe. And we're going to try our best to find the rest of our people. Because—because our best is all we can do."

Tara smiled at him. But more than anything else, Seann smiled at him.

He felt Tara's warmth so close to him. Felt that urge so crystal clear in his chest. That urge to reach over. That urge to hold her hand. That urge to bridge that gap between them.

And then he put a hand on her back.

Pressed it against it. Gently.

Kept it there a few seconds, even though it felt dangerous, and even though it felt scary.

He felt her tuck her head into his shoulder for just a second. Just a second of warmth. Just a second of closeness.

And then he lowered his hand, and Tara moved her head away, and the moment was gone.

They stood there. Stood there at the gates of this community. Stood there at this remains of the NRS—or in the wake of the NRS' destruction. He didn't know which one it was. He couldn't be sure. None of them were probably ever going to be sure.

But that didn't matter. All that mattered now was each other. And all that mattered was trying the best they could. All the damned time.

"Come on," Sam said. Taking a deep breath. "Let's... let's go find our people."

And then they both nodded and walked alongside him into the rising sun.

He didn't know if they'd find their people. He wanted to, but he didn't know. And he couldn't be sure. He didn't know where they were. Didn't know what their situation was. Didn't know what they were going through. If they were going through anything. He didn't know a thing.

But he knew one thing. And it was the only thing that mattered.

Life was completely out of control.

But he could only do his best.

And from this point on, that's exactly what he was going to fucking do.

CHAPTER FIFTY-TWO

Rebecca stopped walking when she saw the walls in the distance.

It was morning. A boiling one, too, like summer was making a final stand. She could taste sweat on her lips and feel her greasy hair clinging to her forehead. It'd been so long since she'd felt fresh. Even when that brief storm hit a few days ago and drenched her, it was nowhere near enough to cleanse her.

But as she stood on the slope and looked down at those walls, everything faded into irrelevance for a moment. The only thing that mattered were those walls. The only thing that mattered was right in front of them. A final endpoint, right at the end of their long, arduous journey.

"What do you think?" A voice. Right beside her. Claude. He stood there, looking pale and more gaunt than he used to. The last month had taken it out of them. *Really* taken it out of them. There were things she didn't want to think about. There were things she didn't want to remember. But at the end of the day... at the end of the day, everyone was still here. Everyone was still standing.

Just about.

She looked past Claude. Looked at Leonard, walking alongside him. She saw the wide expression in her son's eyes as Harvey wagged his tail by his side. She felt so sorry for him. For what he'd been through. For what he'd had to experience. For what he'd had to witness.

She thought of Marky, and her stomach knotted.

"Rebecca?" Claude said.

She jolted back into the moment. Snapped out of her mind and back into the present. But it didn't push the nerves away. It didn't push the fear away. That knot, still tightening in her stomach and her chest, all completely bound to those awful memories.

"What do you think?" Claude repeated.

Rebecca turned back around to the walls in the distance. She looked at the towers. She thought she could see people standing there holding rifles. Watching. She could see gates. She could see all the signs of a community right there in front of her. And yet she felt so nervous. She felt so cautious.

She looked back over her shoulder. Into the woods. And for a second, just a second, she swore she saw a little boy standing between the trees. Watching her.

She swallowed a lump in her throat. Closed her burning, tired eyes. And then she turned back around to face those walls. And to face that community that awaited them right there in the distance.

"Come on," she said. "Let's... let's go check it out."

Claude opened his mouth like he was about to say something. And then he closed his lips again. Nodded. Forced a smile. "We've... we've done good," he said.

Rebecca looked into his eyes, and she saw a flash of what'd happened.

She heard the screams.

She felt the warmth on her hands.

She tasted—

"Hey," Claude said. Stepping closer to her. "We've... we've done the only thing we can. We've done—we've done our best. Always. Right?"

She felt Claude's presence close by. She felt his warmth. She heard his words, and she wanted to believe them. She wanted to believe every single one of them.

But all she could think about were the memories in her mind.

She looked past Claude over at Leonard and Harvey and took a deep breath.

"We've done our best," she said.

And then, together, they walked down the slope towards that community.

They didn't see the letters NRS etched right into the metal on a rusty signpost right by their side.

Or the X scratched right across those letters.

In blood.

END OF BOOK 7

Dawn of Crisis, the eighth book in the World Without Power series, is now available.

If you want to be notified when Ryan Casey's next novel is released—and receive an exclusive post apocalyptic novel totally free—sign up for the author newsletter: ryancaseybooks.com/fanclub